American

Boy

ZARA J.

UNIVERSITY PUBLICATIONS

www.Upublications.com
Twitter: UniversityPub
Facebook: University Publications
Instagram: Universitypublications
Email: Info.universitypublications@gmail.com

ISBN: 978-0991591411
Manufactured in the United States of America

Bismillah

Dear Readers,

Umar and Celine are learning to navigate through life with their unexpected baby on the way. With the return of Tara, Umar's childhood crush, their already rocky relationship now has to face a new hill. Only for Umar having a woman by his side that adheres to the same beliefs tugs at his heart just as much as the guilt of his sins. Will they manage to balance this love triangle?

Writing American Boy was a challenge. Knowing how touchy the subject of Zina (fornication) and children out of wedlock can be for some, I truly tried to paint a realistic picture with the best intentions. These things happen. Should we celebrate them? No. Should we ignore them? No. I pray that anyone who has or currently is facing this dilemma finds encouragement with this novel to right their wrongs and to do better.

Thank you to all that have supported Dowry Divas and other Muslim/Islamic fiction novels. We encourage you to continue to read and share your love for the genre. Please post reviews on social media websites as well as other book platforms such as Amazon and Goodreads. We need your support! Subscribe to our newsletter for giveaways, new releases, and other promotions. Visit our website to subscribe: www.Upublications.com

See you soon,

Zara J.

Facebook: Zara J   Twitter:CEOZaraJ
Instagram: Author_ZaraJ   Email: CeoZaraJ@gmail.com

Loose Translations

As salaamu alaikum/ Wa alaikum salaam- Peace Be to you
Bismillah- In the name of Allah/God
In shaa Allah- Allah/God willing
Masha Allah- Great/Amazing because Allah made it that way
Alhumdullah- All praise and thanks due to Allah
SubhanAllah- Glory be to Allah
Salaat- Muslims offer five daily prayers
Zina- Fornication
Nikkah- Marriage
Na'am- Yes
Laa- No
Masjid/Mosque- Place of worship
Wudu- Washing before prayer
Tawbah- repentance
Gshul- Full body cleansing before prayer
Hijab- Woman's covering

Upcoming releases from University Publications

Khadijah's Got Her Groove by F.A. Ibrahim

Her Justice by Nasheed Jaxson

The Submissive Wife by Zara J.

Now Available by University Publications

Dowry Divas by Zara J.

American Boy by Zara J.

C1

Pregnant? Umar refused to believe his ears. No, he wouldn't believe his ears. Momentarily stunned by the thought of an affluent career dwindling far–far down the grimiest toilet in the city of Philadelphia, Umar stared in utter disbelief at the ivory stick lain on the desk. The tiny window on the device had the nerve to have a pink smiley face ogling at him as if saying–cut the check, *now*. There was absolutely—no way, Celine could've been pregnant. Any minute now a fleet of cameras and coworkers would flock into the cubical cackling, clapping, and the whole shebang screaming the joke was on him–they had to.

"You're just going to sit there with that stupid look on your face, Umar? Say something." He could tell Celine was trying to keep her voice low, but Umar's usual silent response when backed into a corner always seemed to aggravate her.

Celine snatched the pregnancy test from the desk and stuffed it into her six-hundred dollar Coach bag–sprouting Umar's memory of the day she'd bought it. Celine hadn't hesitated to mention the hefty price tag. Instantly, the gaudy cha-ching of coins being withdrawn from Umar's account and deposited into hers rang sharply in his head. What was he thinking–*child support?* That was the least of his worries, for now.

"Umar," she impatiently spat while snapping her manicured gold talons in front of his bewildered face.

"I don't know what you want me to say…um–"

"Celine?"

"Yes, Celine."

"You've forgotten my name?"

"No, of course not. Everything is just moving too fast."

And it was. Just months prior, Celine started her first day as a paid intern at American Muslim Entertainment. Although the majority of the employees were Muslims a few, mainly interns, weren't. Celine fit into that few. After their boss Rashid insisted she'd work under Umar on a Love My Beard celebrity campaign, her inescapable flirting began. Partnering male and females on projects wasn't unusual at AME, they were Equal Opportunity Employers; the problem was for the first time in years Umar struggled with controlling his nafs around a woman. Celine, with her charming Canadian accent and half Cambodian features, was mouthwatering bait for a fish that hadn't eaten in a very long time. Not only did she sneakily wear him down with her form fitting dresses, sweet perfume, and ruby red lipstick that seemingly made her olive skin glow; she eventually wore down his belt as well. Now Umar faced one of his worst fears; a baby out of wed-lock by a woman that didn't practice his same beliefs.

"I'm sorry if this is moving too fast as you put it–but we have to talk about this, Umar. I'm not ready to be a mom. I just graduated from college, and now this? Do you think I should get an abortion?"

"Abortion? Of course not, Celine, I'm Muslim."

Her muddled stare made the hairs on his arms stand. "So?"

"So," he said, "that's just not what we do."

"Well I'm guessing that means you're going to take care of us?"

Slumping his shoulders, Umar contemplated how the next eighteen years would play out. "I have no choice."

"Don't say it like that, Umar. Your child and I aren't a charity case. What do you mean by you don't have a choice? At least sound a little enthused."

"Enthused? Celine, I will uphold my obligations as a man and a Muslim, but please don't expect me to throw a parade over this matter."

Umar shook his head. He was a few projects away from being promoted to head correspondent of Muslim affairs at his company. He'd worked hard for that spot; late nights, red eyes, an outstanding reputation within the community, and he was a damn good dresser. Jobs were pouring in for Umar to act as a guest speaker, or simply hosting appearances at Islamic social events. This would definitely ruin his image.

He cleared his throat. This wasn't going to go over well, but he had to say it.

"You can't tell anyone about this, Celine."

The wrinkles in the corners of her hazel eyes curved as they'd turned to threatening slits. Celine's gaze could slowly burn a hole right through his pupils. *Gosh, she was beautiful.* Her dangerous beauty was exactly what caused the grief he was now experiencing.

"What do you mean *don't tell anyone*, Umar?"

"I have a reputation–"

"Now you want to play good Muslim?"

"It was only one night, Celine. There's no need to be condescending. We both know it was an accident."

"So, I'm an accident?" her voice elevated.

"The baby was," he said, "and yes you were too."

"I can't believe this."

"Believe what?"

"The lack of accountability you're taking for your actions, Umar. I thought so highly of you. There you were a gentle, religious, hardworking man; but now I've come to find out you're just a jerk."

"Whoa, let's not do this right now."

"When would be a better time for you?" she said. Celine was back to waving one of her talons in his face.

"Shhhh," he hushed, scoping out the entry way to his cubicle for onlookers. She was about to cause a scene. "It was an accident let's be realistic. I felt disgusting and ashamed after making ghsul the next morning."

"Ghsul?"

Umar slapped a hand over his eyes and inhaled a deep breath. Her question aggravated him more than the pregnancy. He had no business committing zina. Celine didn't even understand the proper way to cleanse afterward—now he was disgusted with himself even more.

"I'll explain that another time. The point is, I made tawbah—repented," he clarified, "and fasted the next day. So yes, Celine, it was an accident. When it's right you don't have to do all those things."

Celine's lips twisted doubtfully. "I didn't have to do those things," she mockingly retorted, "so it wasn't a mistake. Anyway, Umar, I'm not going to be a top secret baby mama for nine months."

He released a loud, agitated huff. "We'll talk about this later."

She was giving him an intensely throbbing headache. Celine's level of comfortableness with a show-and-tell showcase of their wed-locked child made him quiver. His family would have a heart attack–for certain. He and his brother, Khalid, were first generation Moroccans born on American soil. Already the strong, Islamic foundation they'd been cemented with was jack hammered–thanks to him.

"Umar," Celine said, face smeared with disappointment, "this isn't exactly how I pictured the first time I'd tell a man I was pregnant."

Man, she was right. He was so busy aiding his own insecurities he hadn't bothered to care about hers. Typically, Umar was Mr. Sensitive and very understanding. Celine deserved better treatment than what he'd displayed.

"I apologize, Celine, and I will make it up to you. As long as I'm around you won't have to worry about anything, in shaa Allah."

She smiled bleakly behind cocoa-colored umbrella bangs that accentuated her trendy, chin-length haircut.

"Just keep this between us for now, okay? That's all I'm asking."

Obviously fed-up with Umar's self-centeredness, Celine groaned through a tight-lipped frown and sashayed out of the cubical. He had the feeling his request wouldn't be taken seriously. Celine's spite could put dents in his career that, if Allah willed, would be non-reparable. She needed to keep her mouth shut. If not for him, than for the baby's sake.

C2

The after work crowd piled onto the blue-line subway train at 15th and Market street like a school of fish squeezing into a can. It was humid, sweaty, and noisy in the mobile hotbox, and the earsplitting blare of new age hip-hop from someone's static infused cellphone speakers made Umar's already distressing day elevate a few notches on his pissed-off-o-meter. The only thing on his mind was getting home–pronto. There, in shaa Allah, he'd navigate through YouTube until he'd find a video that soothed his conscience. Although he was a newscaster for AME's video blog Umar wasn't much of a TV watcher, but he did however love a great Islamic lecture.

Celine had to be playing some sort of mind game. No doubt at twenty-six Umar was old enough to have a child, but it wasn't on his agenda. He planned to travel the country interviewing Muslims that were prominent in the community and corresponding for events. So far, he'd moved far up the ladder at AME in the past three years. The company had really taken off thanks to social networks and other internet sites. Umar gained a reputation for being a community activist, and the new IT boy to watch. Blogs, photographers, and spoken word arenas all wanted to feature him–and why not? For being only 5'10, he possessed a well-sculpted physique, creamy suntanned skin, and a head full of luscious chestnut curls. Beyond that, whether in a thobe or a pair of slacks, Umar's style was something to take notes on.

More patrons flooded the train. It seemed like more were coming than going and the little personal space available was quickly being invaded. That's when he saw her.

Tara, Umar's childhood crush, stood near the back of the train more beautiful than he'd remembered. He hadn't seen her since high school; aside from Instagram and other websites. Still, Tara hadn't changed a bit. Her bronze skin had just a touch of makeup, clear lip gloss glistened on her full lips, and she hadn't gained a pound–from what he could tell anyways. Instinctively not wanting to miss the opportunity to reunite, Umar began wedging through the tight crowd, bumping and aggravating each person he passed until he made it to the pole Tara held onto. As soon as she spotted him, her lips parted to a broad crescent.

"As salaamu alaikum, ahki, how have you been?" She sounded beyond elated–a plus for Umar's plans.

"Wa alaikum salaam, Tara, alhumdullah, and you?"

"Alhumdullah," she said. "Don't you look cool in this blazing heat? Red V-neck shirt with camouflage shorts? Hmmm, the look fits you well."

Umar glanced over her pink pastel and green floral long-sleeved dress and matching pink hijab. "Masha Allah, uhkti, your reward is in jannah; the coolness of it beats what I'm feeling today."

"In shaa Allah,"

"Yes," he said, "in shaa Allah."

"What's new, Umar, will you be attending Muslim Day with the 76ers?"

What's new? Besides the unexpected baby he had on the way? Not much. "I'll be there. Actually, I have the opportunity to interview Kareem Khatab. He's the only Muslim on the team."

"Masha Allah, Umar. You are really moving up, alhumdullah. I'm so proud of you."

"Thanks."

Not sure if it was the heat or Tara's kindness, but Umar's cheeks were flushed like candy apples. Tara always had that effect on him. When their families would merge for Eids or other gatherings, Umar would find a way to shy out of the room to avoid staring at her extensively. He should've proposed marriage after graduation. But, Tara married a brother from California that was studying to be an Imam. He couldn't compete with that. Umar attended Islamic schooling his entire life and loved Islam dearly, but he wanted to be a journalist. In his opinion, Tara deserved to be as close to paradise as possible. Good thing for him that marriage didn't last–although, he could never find a sure shot reason why. The divorce rumor mill typically generated information in the blink of an eye. Tara somehow managed to keep her marital issues very low key.

Umar had three more stops to gather as much information as possible. It was time to torpedo her with every question he needed to know. "How long have you been in town?" he asked. "The last I heard you were gallivanting around California, lounging on beaches, and surfing in hijab."

She chortled. "I never surfed, Umar."

"I'd pay to watch." That didn't sound as clean as he intended but it was too late. He flashed his billionaire boy's smile.

"I've been here for a month, waiting for a nursing position to open. For now I'm leeching off my parents in West Philly. They don't seem to mind, though."

"Of course not, I wouldn't mind if I was them." That was a pathetic attempt to win points. Who would want a woman leeching off of them? In any case, Tara appeared to be enjoying his weak banter. Umar grinned. He wanted her–bad.

"Is your husband leeching off your parents too?"

Tara's eyes uncomfortably looked to the left.

"No," she said, "he's still in California."

"Oh ok, I guess he will move when you find a job." He was prying, but Umar was waiting for her to announce the divorce openly so he could further investigate.

Tara, however, ignored his comment.

"Are you married yet?" she asked.

He shook his head.

"Kids?"

"No–not yet. How about you, Tara?"

"I haven't been blessed, yet. I would love to one day, though."

"I'm sure you and your husband will be blessed any day now."

She grinned. Damn. Tara refused to take the bait. She was a master subject avoider of some sort.

"Are you staying in this area?"

"I'm staying in University City, for now."

Now it was Umar's turn to smile. "We're not too far from each other. In shaa Allah, I'll run into you soon," he said, and released his grip from the pole. "My stop is coming."

"Okay," she yelled over the screeching sound of the trains' breaks coming to a halt. "In shaa Allah I'll see you at the basketball game."

He wanted her phone number. If he could listen to Tara's sweet voice talk him to sleep nightly he would sleep like a baby, but he didn't want to be intrusive. Plus, it wasn't proper for him to get so personal with her. Umar messed up with Celine, Tara was not an option. Besides, he needed to figure out what he and Celine planned to do. His guess, he'd have to marry her. In Umar's eyes, the realization that proposing to Tara had been yanked away, once again, meant Umar's punishment was just beginning.

C3

Swallowing an ample amount of red wine, Celine rifled through her tired wardrobe in search of the perfect dress. Life as a baby mama was exactly how Celine had pictured it–lonely, shameful, and depressing. Growing up in Toronto with her semi-Catholic, Cambodian mother the day to day struggle of watching her mother raise three children solo was anything but picture perfect. Her father had abandoned Celine and her younger siblings at an age too young for her to remember.

Celine's precious baby wouldn't endure the type of desertion she'd experienced. No. She'd spare any child she'd birth from the devastating rejection of growing up fatherless. Umar was going to be super-dad–as long as she was around.

The only problem was Umar had to travel to Virginia for a weekend to press cover for an Islamic conference and was MIA from work ever since she'd dropped the baby-bombshell. He hadn't called or messaged her for days. Not even a simple text to make sure Celine and the baby were okay. Of course, Celine was barely carrying a fetus–but that wasn't the point. The last she'd heard of her disappearing donor was that he'd needed to clear his head, and that they'd talk once he'd returned home.

Thank goodness for her friends Bella and Angelique. They'd promised to take Celine out to get her mind off Umar's *this baby is a scandal* notion. Now all she needed was the perfect scantily clad dress to fit the grand opening for Yellow Lace. Baby-bearing or not, Celine would not miss Philadelphia's premier club red carpet event. Everybody that was somebody was destined to attend, and the pictures would be perfect for her rising entertainment blog. Celine's Cuisine had all the media dirt that a blogger of her statue could dish, but it was time to step it up. In nine months she'd be boggled down with a gorgeous bundle of joy and there was a high chance her well cut curves would expand to twice their size. There was only a short stint for Celine to make a name for herself in the city, and today was the first day of her new campaign. Umar had a reputation to protect? Hmph, so did she.

Deciding on a little black number, Celine ripped the dress from its hanger, added a full face of MAC makeup—with her usual smoky eye routine, and slid into a sleek pair of banana-yellow Vince Camuto pumps. Feeling like a star, Celine strutted out of her apartment building, and headed to the subway.

After smoozing a bouncer Celine became fairly familiar with from VIP hopping, she'd bypassed the velvet rope and entered the club. The extravagant venue was right up Celine's alley. Yellow lights flashed in the dim lighting, while drapes made of eye-catching yellow lace hung from the high ceilings sectioning off areas of the club. For now, a mix of hip-hop and house music blasted through tall speakers. However, before Celine slithered her way through the tight crowd to the VIP area where Angelique and Bella were waiting, the music transitioned to reggae. Yellow Lace definitely had a successful grand opening. By the looks of it, the posh VIP area was flooded with local celebrities, basketball players, and even the well-known Clyde family of Orange County, New Jersey.

"Celine," Angelique screamed, waving for her to hurry to the table.

"Hey girl," she yelled back, quickening her pace. The spilled drinks on the floor made it hard to navigate without slipping, but Celine managed to do so. Then she gently slid onto the cushioned bench and fluffed her hair.

"How's my baby doing?" Bella questioned with her usual puckered lip pout that gave her the slight appearance of a freckled-faced, blue-eyed, blonde-haired duck. She then reached her hand out to rub Celine's non-existent baby-bump, which Celine hastily slapped away.

"Don't embarrass me," she snippily spat.

"Okay, Celine-pooh. Don't be so hormonal. I just wanted to feel my little God-baby. You know I want first dibs on that position."

From the corner of her eyes Celine glared distrustfully at Bella. There wasn't a chance Bella would ever be her darling baby's God parent. Celine wouldn't trust Bella with her favorite handbag. She was an irresponsible alcoholic; smart as a whip but an alcoholic, nonetheless. Bella didn't detach from a bottle of wine unless she was at work.

"Well, I have to discuss Godparents with Umar, but I'm sure he wouldn't mind."

Bella wore a drunken simper that implied she approved Celine's statement.

"Speaking of Umar, what did he say?" Angelique interjected.

Automatically, both of the young women leaned in closely to Celine anticipating a heap of gossip. There meddlesomeness was bothersome, but who was Celine to turn her nose up? She was a gossip blogger for Pete sake. A good dish over a cup of tea–or wine for this matter; always surged a jolt of delight.

"He told me to keep it a secret."

They gasped.

"All of a sudden Umar is like–Mr. Holy, and whatnot. I was totally turned off."

The two women cooed and nodded.

"So are you getting an abortion?" Angelique asked. Her brows pushed together creating a sympathetic frown.

"He's against that. Apparently it's against his religion, or something. He plans to take care of us."

Angelique's frown lifted to a smile, lighting up her toffee skin tone and bright brown eyes. "You know," she said "they tend to marry women quickly. OMG, you're going to be a bride!"

That's when Bella gasped sharply just before tossing the rest of the wine in her glass down her throat. Her glassy sea-blue eyes popped in the dim light. "Does that mean you're becoming a Muslim?" The question reeked of disdain.

Celine hadn't thought about that. She didn't have an interest in being Muslim. Heck, in twenty-four years she'd barely had her fingers wrapped around being Catholic. Too many changes were occurring in such a short amount of time. Quickly pouring a tall glass of wine into one of the empty glasses on the table, Celine took a gulp, and made her decision.

"No. He accepted me how I am; I don't have to change anything. If anything, he should be changing to suit my needs. I'm the one carrying the baby. All he has to do is show up."

They all nodded.

"Besides, if Umar has a problem I can handle the baby by myself."

"That's right, girl, you don't need him," Bella chimed, "We have your back."

"I know you do."

"I dated a Muslim before," Angelique said, "but he wasn't all religious like Umar, thank goodness. I don't know what I would've done if I got pregnant."

Celine rolled her eyes. What a way to make her feel better? Him being Muslim was the least of her concerns. All Celine cared about was not having to raise a child on her own.

"Well Muslim or not, Umar has promised to stick by my side. I'm not sure if we're getting married, yet, but I'm not opposed to it. We just need to get to know each other better."

Bella laughed in a way that tore at Celine's confidence. "Get to know each other better? You guys are having a baby, Celine. I think you know each other pretty well. Now is not the time to focus on getting to know each other. You guys need to plan for the future, and doing so means planning a wedding. You need to secure your spot in his life."

"Hmmm, maybe you're right."

"Of course I am."

"But like we said," Angelique reiterated, "we have your back just in case Umar takes a sudden trip to Morocco."

They all laughed.

"He was born in the United States, Ange, unlike me."

"Either way," she said, "we're here for you."

Even if they weren't, Celine's mind was made. Umar wasn't going to cover her up and ruin her way of life. She was too cute for that. If there was going to be a wedding it would be on her terms—only. With that thought, Celine finished her wine, and then moved onto another.

———————

A few glasses and hours later, Angelique drove up to Celine's apartment door, let her out, and peeled off. Had Celine known she'd end the night so drunk–she would've stayed home. She wasn't concerned about the baby. A few months prior Celine stumbled across an article while waiting for her turn at the nail salon about drinking red wine while pregnant. It was early in the pregnancy and perfectly safe, from what she could remember. In any case, this would be her last night to party hard for the next nine months. She deserved it.

Feet throbbing and with a bladder on the verge of explosion, Celine waddled around the corner to the backside of the building. There was no time to fish for her house keys and tread up the stairs to her apartment. She had to go–now. One final glance to assure privacy; Celine surveyed the alley, lifted her dress, clenched her eyes together and released.

Moments later, in the midst of the much needed relief, a bright light shone on Celine's face practically blinding her. Instinctively blocking her face while scooting down her dress, she turned away from the flashers fixated on her embarrassed scowl.

"Police," a man's voice barked. "You are vandalizing private property."

Damn! What were the chances the police would bust her potty-party? Out of all the times Celine visited the spot after late partying, the one night she was drunk out of her mind the cops showed up? Straightening her posture and squaring her shoulders, Celine made her best attempt to appear sober.

"I live in the building," she yelled back. "I really had to go. Sorry, it won't happen again."

"Does that give you permission to urinate on public property?" Another voice yelled.

"Of course not," she stammered. "I'm sincerely sorry, officers. I promise it won't happen again." She flashed an innocent smile and took a step forward.

"Don't move," the second officer barked threateningly.

Both car doors opened and two officers exited the vehicle. From the driver's side stepped a man. From the passenger's side however, stepped a pint-sized woman with the strut of a soldier. Celine angrily rolled her eyes and shook her head the moment she spotted the mini-bulldog; this was not going to be good.

The two marched in Celine's direction, never withdrawing the annoying light, and stopped about a foot-length's away.

Peering suspiciously into her eyes, the female officer sneered. "You've been drinking?" It was more of a statement than a question.

"Just a few glasses of wine."

"A few, huh?"

Celine nodded.

"Give her a sobriety test," she ordered the male officer whom didn't seem to have the heart to challenge her authority.

"Is that necessary? I had to go to the bathroom and I live upstairs."

The cold-hearted officer shrugged her butch shoulders indifferent to Celine's plea. "Ma'am, you are vandalizing private property, and your insubordination is displaying public drunkenness."

"This is ridiculous."

"Oh is it?" she snickered. "If you are refusing we can take you straight to the district. Is that what you want?"

The other officer returned from the car toting a Breathalyzer. Celine could feel vomit working its way from her stomach to her throat, but she held it down–that would certainly give her away. She wasn't going to pass the test–that was for sure. What also was for sure was that Celine was Canadian; not a US citizen. The last thing she needed right now was a felony charge that could possibly get her deported.

C4

Umar carefully rolled his prayer rug, opened the back door to his silver 2012 Dodge Avenger, and tossed the rug in the backseat. Salaat was good. To Umar's surprise, his focus appeared to have been more intense since the day the news unfolded about fatherhood. Having such loathsome thoughts towards his child and Celine was something he hated, but a part of him couldn't help it. This was not in his plans. A pinch in his ribs told him that Celine set him up and that getting pregnant was in her plans the entire time. Why else would she have seduced him the way she did? She was on a mission.

Once again, Umar a shook the dreadful thoughts from his mind and walked to the driver's side of the car, sat inside, and shut the door. He needed to dump his load onto someone else. Driving back from Virginia was somewhat soothing. Still, the fact that once Umar arrived in Philadelphia he'd be forced to face his new life still lingered like the taunting sound of a winding jack-in-the-box, driving his anticipation of an explosively unpredictable pop that he couldn't avoid. He couldn't shake his anxious thoughts. If Umar could've stayed at the conference a few more days maybe he would've released some more of his stress. The summery VA weather was relaxing and the countryside mixed with the ambush of trees aligning the highway had a classic commercial good ole American appeal. It was the perfect getaway—the slow life. Umar had been spending too much time trying to keep up with the fast lane. Finally—he'd crashed.

No, to some a baby wasn't a big deal—and perhaps it wasn't, but Umar feared change. Celine was unpredictable and had a very carefree way of thinking. The strong stench of drama could already be smelled brewing.

Khalid was the only one that would understand. Although his younger brother usually wasn't much help with life matters, Umar knew he could trust him. Plus, he was far from perfect. Discussing his personal life with some of his more pretentious friends was bound to be a shame-fest. And his less religious, non-Muslim friends already had children or didn't even consider the thought of marriage, so looking for guidance from them was useless. At times he questioned if they secretly loved drama anyways.

With the fleet of depressing and uncertain thoughts swirling in his head, Umar picked up his cell phone and dialed his brother. Advice from Khalid would alleviate some of the stress, in shaa Allah.

"As salaamu alaikum," Khalid's voice came through the car's speakers with a loud echo.

"Wa alaikum salaam."

"How was Virginia?"

"Good, alhumdillah. There was a spoken word competition that was the best I'd ever seen. It felt like I was at a concert; music, drums, and all kinds of lights to bring on the effects. And ya know, with my hosting skills the crowd was excited and cheering like a grudge match. You should've come along."

"Masha Allah," Khalid replied flatly. "I would've come with you but I had some matters to tend to."

"Is everything okay?"

There was a pause before Khalid continued. "You know how I told you I'd gone to the Sugar House a few times lately?"

Umar settled into his seat and tried to focus on the road, but already he was irritated with where this conversation was headed. "Yes?"

"Well, I lost some money–a lot of money, Umar. I'm really behind on my rent."

"What are you doing gambling?" he shrugged unaffected by his brother's desperation. "I don't know what to tell you. Out of nowhere you've developed the habit. You know better."

"I know,"

"So why are you lying?"

"Lying?" Umar's shocking accusation raised Khalid's voice to a high-pitch croak.

"I'm not stupid, Khalid. You lost your rent money? That means you've been down there more than a few times, and this has been going on for more than a few weeks."

Khalid blew a hard breath into the phone but didn't object.

"Did you tell abu?"

"Laa,"

"Ummi?"

"Umar, I'm telling you. Isn't that enough?"

"No because I can't help you." His callous discord was not to be taken lightly.

A call was coming through on Umar's other line. He leered at the unknown number and ended the call.

"Umar, let me stay with you for a few months until I save up enough money for a new place?"

"No."

"Are you serious?"

First Celine and now Khalid. Umar's temples were drumming up to a weak throb as he thought about the people out to sabotage his life.

"Wine and gambling go hand in hand. In them both lies grave sin."

"Na'am, which is why I need your help. Are you going to deny your brother help and shelter?"

"Don't guilt me."

"I'm not, Umar, but I just need it temporarily."

Hesitantly, Umar muttered, "Okay."

Khalid was more responsible than this. Ever since he'd left for college new layers of Khalid's life were being added on. First there was the bottle of wine Umar found behind the sofa next to the hookah in his brother's apartment. Then it was him lagging with prayers and attending jummuah. However gambling–and his rent money at that, displayed Khalid being nowhere near the sound Muslim he was raised to be. They both needed a wakeup call. As disappointed as Umar was, he had no room to criticize– his sin had a longer-lasting effect.

The same unknown number called again. Umar quickly ended the call. He was sure it was Celine playing one of her games, again. She'd been calling from random numbers during his stay in Virginia whenever he refused to answer her calls. Umar was being rude, but he needed space and time to think. If she had any sense at all she'd give him that.

"When will you be moving in? You'll have to sleep on the sofa or buy an air mattress. And I'm only giving you three months. I won't charge you any rent. Just promise to get back on track."

"Alhumdullah, shukron Umar. Jazaakallahu kyhr."

"Afwan, wa 'iyyakum."

Another nagging call came through which instantly sent Umar's blood to a steaming boil. Celine and Khalid had his ill-temper ready to burst through. *Sabr.* Quickly reasoning with himself, Umar took a deep inhale and silently asked Allah to help him with his patience and understanding.

Slowly he pressed on the brake pedal. DC traffic was miserable and always seemed to come to a halt. Umar relaxed into the cushioned seat and ran his fingers through his thick, head of curls.

"Since you're going to be staying at my house I should tell you about Celine."

"The cute intern at your job?"

"Yes," Umar mumbled, "her."

"What about her?"

"She's pregnant," he blurted.

"By who?"

"Who else would she be pregnant by, Khalid? If it was the mailman I wouldn't waste my time telling you, now would I?"

"Relax Umar, it was a question."

"I just don't have a lot of patience right now." Hotly, he gazed into traffic; it wasn't going to move anytime soon. "I'm trying to talk to you about the matter and I'm already ruffled."

"You and that fuse."

"I'm trying to help it."

"It's understandable. That's how those grave sins will have you." Khalid's jab was uneventful. Umar had too much on his mind to care. "What now?"

"What else? I wanted to give you a heads up in case she ever pops up at the apartment. I mean, she seems okay, but I really don't know her too well."

"When are you going to tell the parents?"

Umar shook his head. It was kind of pathetic how he still feared telling his parents the earnest truth about situations, but it was out of respect. His father was a very conservative Muslim, and his mother was even more reserved than his father. This felt like childhood all over again. Anything that Umar did that was a bad reflection of the family made him feel extremely guilty. Their family's reputation meant the world to his parents. They prided themselves on honor and dignity; somehow both of their sons lacked in those areas.

"I think I'll wait to make sure the baby will be healthy before telling them. A lot of women miscarry. There isn't a need to ruffle their feathers and the baby doesn't make it."

"It sounds like that's what you're hoping for." Khalid had the audacity to sound disgusted with Umar's regard.

Umar sneered at the speaker as if Khalid could see his disdain. Honestly, it would've been a lie if said thoughts of Celine losing the baby never crossed his mind. It was wrong, but he really didn't like the idea of having a child with a woman that not only shared a different belief, but wasn't even his wife. It was one big accident.

The unknown number called again. Just like before, he ended the call. Celine could wait until he got back to Philadelphia.

C5

Celine slammed the phone onto the receiver oozing with frustration. Umar was refusing to answer her calls. She had no clue as to what she could've done to make him so furious with her, but what she did know was she needed him to help pay her bail. It was a small nine-hundred dollar fine, but she knew her mother hadn't the resources to send the money. Not to mention her petty bank account only accumulated a small monthly savings. Sadly, after all of the shopping, clubbing, and trips to the nail salon, Celine hadn't two pennies to rub together.

The mini pit bull of a woman that arrested her snarled at Celine, keeping her glare on her as she placed the phone on the hook. For whatever reason, the woman really had it out for Celine. Crude remarks about Celine's accent and how the oh-so-pretty little woman just knew she could break the law and get away with it constantly surged from the officer's lips. She needed to get out of the small jail cell–now. It was cold, filthy, and packed with prostitutes and other low-lives from the city. Foul odors from the zombie-like women permeated her nostrils almost causing Celine to vomit while scrunched in the cell, fortunately she forcefully held it down. Vomit would've only added to the pungent smells. Celine couldn't imagine what the actual prison must've been like. Scorned by the unfair punishment she'd received for not being able to hold her bladder the night before, and the refusal to spend another day in a holding cell, Celine swallowed her pride and grinned a wan smile at the female officer.

"Ma'am, can I please make another call?"

"You can't keep using the phone. You're not the only person in here, ya know, darling?" She spit her sarcastic retort with a daggered glare.

Celine cracked her knuckles and forged a grin. "You're correct, ma'am, but I can't get in contact with anyone and I'm pregnant. Please," she said "can I make another call?"

The woman pursed her lips crookedly and looked Celine over from head to toe. "Pregnant and drinking? Hmph."

"It was a mistake. One I will never make again."

"That holding cell is filled with women that would, never do it again." She snorted a smug chuckle that almost aroused Celine's fist to lunge across the desk and clamber her canine mug.

"Please? This really was just a one night thing."

The woman gave another glance over. "I guess," she said, as if it pained her to do so.

"Thanks."

Celine promptly dialed Bella's number. The phone rang about six times before Bella finally answered with a curious hello. There wasn't time for idle chitchat. Knowing the guard dog-officer was watching, Celine hastily got to the point.

"Bella, I got into some trouble I need you to bail me out of jail."

"What?"

"I know–I know, I'll go into details later. This little arrest could cause a major problem."

"How much do you need?"

"Nine-hundred dollars," she reluctantly replied.

"Ouch, Celine-pooh, I don't have that kind of money to throw away."

"Yeah, I kind of figured."

"But I can't allow my God baby to rot in prison. I'll call Angelique and see what we can scrape together."

"Thanks Bella."

"No problem. Did you ask Umar for help?"

This was the idle talk that Celine purposefully wanted to avoid.

"I can't get through to him."

"Good."

"Huh?"

"Knowing Umar he would make you feel awful for being human, and you don't need that right now. Let's just handle the matter and tuck this little problem away. It will disappear in no time."

That would be perfect, but it wasn't realistic. Eventually Celine would have to get a lawyer to make sure her student Visa wouldn't be compromised. But once again, there wasn't time to discuss that matter.

"Maybe you're right. I don't like keeping secrets but this situation is stressful enough. I don't need to feel any worst."

"Exactly, Celine-pooh. Like I told you at the club, I have your back."

Celine hurriedly gave Bella the station information and told her to head to 13th and Filbert street to pay the bail as soon as possible. Bella assured her that the she'd handle the matter and warned her once again not to tell Umar.

"And another thing," Bella stated before ending the call, "I'll need you to pay the money back. I don't mind helping a friend in need but I can't afford to lose a couple hundred dollars."

Celine was rolled her eyes, and said through a tightened jaw, "I understand."

"Great."

Some friend she was. There were plenty of times Celine had given Bella money to assist with bills and never asked for the money back. Celine had a baby on the way. Now added to the list was the burden of fines and other lawful matters. Bella had the nerve to tell her to pay back a few hundred dollars? Tough luck! Celine had enough problems on her plate. Being in debt to a so-called friend wasn't one of them.

"Just get down here as quickly as possible, please?"

"Okay, Celine-pooh, I'm on my way."

C6

Tara. She had been on Umar's mind from the moment he crossed the Pennsylvania state line and entered his apartment an hour ago. He wanted to see her–bad, but that wouldn't be possible. Telling Tara about Celine was not an option. Tara was the kind of woman he'd marry, but with Celine being pregnant the likelihood of that happening was slim.

Turning onto his side on the king sized bed topped with sporty red, white, and blue plaid bedding, Umar shuffled through his Instagram page in search of Tara's profile. Moonstruck, he smiled. Tara updated her profile to a picture she'd must've taken the day they'd ran into each other. She wore the same floral outfit and hijab, and her smile was just as broad and inviting as he remembered it. Celine was hot—Tara was beautiful. He loved her modesty and the way she managed to evoke style and confidence while covering. On top of that Tara was intelligent, well-mannered, and had flawless brown skin. She wore very little makeup which also increased his desire for her natural beauty. Celine plastered the crap on like a clay mold.

Without another thought, Umar sent Tara a direct picture with the message as salaamu alaikum call me please with his number attached. To his surprise, she'd instantly replied back returning the salaams and her number. This was perfect. Umar had a sudden boost in confidence. Tara was interested enough to offer her number. He may have had a chance after all.

"As salaamu alaikum," Tara answered.

"Wa alaikum salaam, Tara, how are you?"

"I'm okay. How about you, Umar?"

"Now that I'm talking to you," he said, "wonderful."

She released a light-hearted giggle. "Masha Allah, Umar, you're such a gentleman. I was surprised to see your message."

"Why is that?"

"Oh ya know, you're just Mr. popularity these days. I didn't think I would cross your mind."

"Tara, how could you not cross my mind? Actually, you've been on my mind since the day I saw you on the train."

"Really?" He could tell she was smiling by the elevation in her pitch.

"Yup, you've invaded my thoughts consistently. I've tried to push you out of them, but man, you're smile is hypnotic."

"That doesn't sound too good."

Her flirtatious tone had Umar's grin beaming radiantly.

"It's very good. Can I be upfront with you Tara? I called for a reason."

"And what's that?"

"Well," he said, "are you looking to get married again? I'm asking because I really think you're beautiful and I wouldn't mind being a runner-up."

Tara chuckled again then cleared her throat. "I wouldn't mind marrying again to the right man."

"What makes someone the right man?"

She hummed. "You'll have to ask my father," she said.

"That's fair. Are you able to spot a bad one?"

"Sometimes I'm not so sure." All enthusiasm fled her tone.

The reason behind Tara's divorce had to be on the tip of her tongue. Umar decided to press forward with the interrogation. If he had a chance with her, he needed to make sure she wasn't crazy or if she was simply worth his time.

"So what was wrong with your husband?"

Tara was silent for a brief stint. Apparently juggling with the proper way to relay the information, or even if she should reveal it to Umar, Tara released a dejected sigh.

"It was me not him," she finally admitted.

"That's a shock."

"It shouldn't be," she said more defensively than expected, "Umar, I'm not perfect."

He sat upright and adjusted himself to a comfortable position.

"I didn't mean to upset you."

"You didn't. It's just a sensitive subject."

"Hey if you don't want to talk about it I understand. We all have skeletons in our closets. I'm more interested if those skeletons would affect you and I."

"Is there a, *you and I*, Umar?"

Now he felt silly. Of course there wasn't a, *you and I*. This was their first real conversation in years. He'd gotten ahead of himself even fixing his lips to blurt such a ridiculous phrase. Tara hadn't even hinted If she was interested in him. For all he knew she was simply being friendly–nothing more. Then again, he was Umar Talb–what woman wouldn't want to be on his arm?

"In shaa Allah," Umar announced the term suavely.

"In shaa Allah."

He decided to allow her to bypass his onset of questioning—for now. They had plenty of time to get to the nitty-gritty of why her marriage didn't work, and why Tara considered it to be her fault. Currently, Umar wanted to enjoy having her to talk to. Who knew how long he'd be able to get away with keeping the baby a secret. The way Umar saw it, if he could win Tara over she'd look past his mistake. Good women did that—that's what he'd noticed in his friends' marriages. Tara seemed to be a forgiving person, from what he could remember, anyways. Besides, she willingly admitted to not being perfect. Why would she expect him to be?

"How about you get your wakil and let me give you a night to remember?"

C7

Crashing her handbag onto the kitchen counter, Celine sauntered over to the refrigerator, yanked open its door, and removed her Brita from the fridge. She'd been dying for a refreshing glass of cold water all weekend. The food and beverages she'd been served were hardly appeasing to her appetite. The sandwich was smashed, the drink was too sugary for her taste, and considering the condition of the holding cell she wasn't too enthused about eating in such a horrid chamber.

On top of it all, Celine had morning sickness. This just hadn't been her week. And where was Umar? When she did catch up to him Celine planned to be hell in heels. He'd abandoned her. More than likely he was somewhere gallivanting with his nose in the air pretending to be some goody-two-shoes–which was far from the truth. Hmph! It seemed as if Celine was going to have to remind him just how flawed he really was.

"Do you need me to stay with you? It's not a problem. I really don't want to leave you alone with you throwing up and all," Bella said.

To think, the walking bottle of wine pitied Celine, oh please! Umar would certainly answer for not being available at such a crucial moment and making her out to be someone else's burden.

She poured Bella a glass of water as well. "I'd really appreciate it if you would, Bella. I've never been so sick."

"I see," she said with a crumpled frown. "I could barely stomach seeing you hanging over the side of the car myself."

Ignoring her displeasure, Celine walked to Bella, handed her the glass, and flopped down on her less-than comfortable orange sofa. She hated the hard cushioned piece of furniture, but with her college loans digging deep into her finances it was all she could afford. Besides, she'd rather spend the money on a pair of shoes or a trendy handbag, not an item for other people to rest their rumps on. Student loans. Celine was suddenly reminded of the disclaimer on her loan applications. Getting a felony charge would not only possibly affect her Visa, but it could also cut off ties of funding with her financial institution. This was a disaster! The urge to vomit churned in her gut. Too many emotions, too many consequences, and too many lucid smells from the ride from the prison to her home.

Feeling flushed with nausea and a fluttering heartbeat, Celine took a gulp of air and attempted to hold down the water she'd just finished devouring.

"Are you okay?" Bella asked.

She nodded.

"Okay because you look as if—"

Celine sprung to her feet and darted to the bathroom. What little food and water still left in her system plummeted into the toilet. At that point, she broke into a downpour of tears. Seated crossed-legged on the tiled bathroom floor, Celine sulked hysterically over the mess her life was transforming into.

When she looked up Bella was angled against the doorway with a sympathetic frown. Bella then wet a wash rag with warm water, kneeled down, and lovingly wiped Celine's tears away.

The warm cloth comforted Celine right away. She gently cleaned Celine's face then wiped her mouth with a swooping motion. This wasn't a side of Bella Celine was not used to seeing. Bella was almost–motherly, you could say. Celine had to admit, despite her demand of repayment for the bail money Bella really was a good friend. And at this point, her only true support system. With the assistance of Bella pulling her to her feet, Celine stood, then re-entered the living room.

"Did you check your cell phone?" Bella asked.

She assumed Bella's question was in reference to seeing if Umar had called. Celine shook her head. She didn't want to check to see. Had she viewed a slew a missed calls, and Umar not being one of them, it may have sent her into a frantic rage. It would've been better to wait until she'd calmed down–and was alone. The situation was embarrassing enough.

"I called out of work for the next two days," Celine said, "I really just want to rest and have peace and quiet. I'll deal with Umar then."

"I hope you do," Bella snipped, now back to her normal brash-self, nodded her head like a stoop pigeon. "He certainly deserves a taste of his own medicine. How dare he leave my Celine-pooh in jail?" Bella's tone was extremely exaggerated. However, it had Celine engulfed with the encouragement of revenge.

"I wouldn't have it any other way, Bella. In fact, he'll be interviewing some basketball player at the Muslim Day 76ers game. I think I'll make a guest appearance."

Bella wore a devilish grin that screamed payback. "That sounds like fun."

"Now we can't go too far," Celine stammered, "remember he and I work for the same company."

Bella nodded.

"But I have an idea that will at least remind Umar that for the next nine months–I am his priority."

8

When Umar's boss Rashid first called him into the office he'd thought he would be a part of one of his long-winded pep talks that usually motivated Umar to get the ball rolling on his acting career. However, the wrinkled frown on Rashid's face hinted otherwise. He was seated on the corner of his Maplewood desk in a simple black t-shirt and off-white slacks, snacking on a glazed donut with a steaming cup of coffee clasped in his hand. He looked bothered–very perplexed. Leisurely nibbling on his bottom lip, Rashid focused in on Umar with a questionable sneer. Unsure what to make of the stressed look on Rashid's face, Umar sat slouched patiently adjacent to his boss. At the moment Rashid was bound to say anything, and at the top of Umar's dreaded list was that Rashid caught wind of one of the work place laws that he'd broken–fraternizing with interns.

Rashid, only three years older than Umar yet far more successful, was a huge fan and supporter of Umar's charisma and ability to entertain. It was Rashid that encouraged Umar to be on the forefront of American Muslim Entertainment. Prior, Umar was a mere paper pusher with the gift of gab and a great sense of humor; but Rashid spotted more. In just a few months of working for the company, Rashid promoted Umar to a correspondent, and in little to no time Umar was the featured host for many of the company's events, his video blog for AME took off tremendously, and he'd mastered the ability to become likeable to the masses. With the blessing of Allah, and a little help from Rashid, the last three years of Umar's life had taken off in a way he'd never imagined. The popularity was humbling. Although he enjoyed the spotlight, Umar knew that becoming arrogant would ruin his image and blessings. Ironically, Umar focused so intensely on not allowing arrogance to be his weakness that he overlooked all of the other matters lurking into his lifestyle.

"Brother," Rashid started and placed the cup on the desk, "I want to talk to you about something."

"Is something wrong?" Whenever Rashid referred to Umar as brother there was always something wrong.

"I wouldn't say that," he said.

"So what's up?"

"There's been some rumors floating around the office."

Umar shifted uneasily in the hard wooden chair. "Like what?"

"Nothing for you to worry about," Rashid lifted and eyebrow and glared, "at least to my knowledge. I think it's all gossip, ya know, typical women's talk. It seems as if some of the female workers are feeling uncomfortable with the policies of allowing opposite sexes to work on projects."

Umar, feeling flushed with relief, relaxed his rattled nerves and straightened his posture to a more respectable position.

"That doesn't seem like much to worry about. I'm surprised it's the women that feel that way."

"Isn't it always?"

They both chuckled.

"You can't please them," Rashid continued. "Give them too many rights they want it more conservative. If you don't give them enough they're ready to burn clothing and march with signs about women's rights. I say we draw from a hat daily." Rashid used his hands to demonstrate a ticket withdrawing. "Today we are conservative tomorrow we are liberal."

Umar laughed. Rashid certainly had a point. "And then they will say every day we are Muslim."

"SubhanAllah," Rashid blurted. "This is true. Yet, we have to make everyone comfortable. I'm trying my best to run a respectable Islamic business, Umar, I really am. How do I find the balance that allows me not to exclude qualified candidates? This is America. I can't say you're not welcome to practice here due to your beliefs, it's not right. I know I wouldn't want that. If I needed to work for a Jewish media company as a camera man then I'd do just that to keep a roof over my head. Should I expect anything less from those that apply to work here?"

Umar sat quietly. Finding the balance between Islam and society was always a struggle. The goal was to please Allah, that was for sure. Now running a lucrative business and employing those that didn't always feel the same as he, Umar didn't want any parts of that. He was perfectly okay with the lack of corporate responsibility he possessed. Rashid could have it. Just give him a microphone, camera, and a good environment and he'd deliver his part of the equation. Besides that, Umar didn't have any advice to give.

Finally, after a short-lived moment of silence Umar replied, "Allahu alim."

"Na'am Allahu alim, Umar." Rashid's tone was slightly somber and reeked of stress. "This wasn't really what I wanted to talk to you about."

"Oh?"

"No. I want to help you."

"How so?"

The distressed look on Rashid's face vanished and was replaced with a self-assured grin. This was the brother Umar was used to seeing. Rashid's wheels were turning with excitement–it showed all over his face, and knowing the idea was in Umar's favor sent a spurt of eagerness throughout his own vessels.

"As your manager."

Umar burst into a doubtful chortle. "Manager? Manage what?"

"You?"

"Me?" Umar laughed again. "You're already my boss. What more do you expect to do?"

"Make you more money."

"Your hands are already deep into my pockets; you and Uncle Sam's."

"Well I'm trying to dig them deeper, Umar, if you'd give me a chance."

They both laughed.

"Now listen I'm being serious. Yes, you do work for AME; and you do an excellent job; which is exactly why you need to take things to the next level. I told you before, people are watching you."

"So you tell me."

"So I know." Rashid stood from his desk and walked around to Umar's chair. He sat in the seat next to Umar and folded his fingers into one another, placing his fist on the enclave. Hunched over with his broad shoulders squared and aimed, Rashid reminded him of a younger Denzel Washington. This was training day and Umar didn't have much of a choice but to get on board. "It's time to broaden your audience. Your blog on AME has done exceedingly well. You have a name and reputation that speaks for itself. People love and respect you and the Muslims support you. I decided to forward your media kit and some other samplings of your work to the Sports Federation Network."

"And?"

"And they think you'd be a great fit."

Umar couldn't believe it. AME was a great place to work but the Sports Federation Network was major. Mainstream. His face would be shown all over the United States on major media streams. He would be on national television. With the right amount of hard work and an ample amount of blessings, Umar could become the next big thing, in shaa Allah.

Umar was on the edge of his seat like a puppy wagging his tail. This was incredible news. "So what now?"

"Now what you need to do is bomb the 76ers interview. Show the network you'd be a great sportscaster. They're looking forward to seeing more. I think they'd love to have you on their team."

"Rashid I can't think you enough."

"Thank Allah."

"Alhumdullah," Umar gleefully retorted.

"Alhumdullah."

Both men shook hands and Umar stood. He didn't know who to share this news with. His brother Khalid, perhaps? He didn't want to get anyone's hopes too high, but he needed duas—now. Khalid at least would be supportive of his possible promotion.

Just as Umar turned on his heels Rashid called his attention.

"Yes?"

"SFN is looking to expand to Africa to interview some of the prominent soccer and other sport players there. Being that you're Moroccan and Muslim, you'd seem like a good fit for what they're trying to do. I agreed. Just keep in mind if you get the job you'll have to travel out the country, a lot–possibly live there. Give it deep thought before you jump on board. It will be a life changing decision, in shaa Allah, pray ishkitara."

That quickly Umar was knocked off his rocker. Was he ready to move out of America? Sure his parents were from Africa, but he was a red-blooded American. This was definitely something to take to the rug.

The walk back to his cubicle was nothing more than a whirlwind of thoughts. He couldn't wrap his head around all of the different ways his life was being tugged. He wanted to work for SFN. Heck, he needed to. The pay increase would give him the stability he needed for his future family. Family. Celine. Umar stopped in his tracks and looked over his shoulder in the direction of Celine's work area. He hadn't remembered seeing her at work. In fact, he was so wrapped up he didn't remember the last time he saw or spoke with her.

Umar strolled to Celine's partition and peeked inside. It appeared untouched. Had Celine been to work that day a slew of coffee cups and candy wrappers would've been strewn on her desk, accompanied by pop music and her off-key singing. He should check on her. Then again, checking on her would've prompted him to embark in a serious conversation about all that was to come.

No, he wasn't ready for that. Tomorrow was the basketball game and he needed to be on his A-game in order to seal the deal with SFN. He'd call her tomorrow—if she didn't show up to work. On top of it all, he needed a game plan. Celine could be conniving and he didn't need to be swayed towards her wants. Before he'd discuss anything with her she needed to know and understand that whatever he said is exactly what it would be. By now, in shaa Allah, she would've gained some sensibility and learned to talk rationally. He didn't want any drama. If they were to raise the child together they'd do it as a family. She needed to learn and respect Islam. If not, Tara would surely have a place in the running.

C9

"Long time no see." Ishmil Tara's older brother said after shaking hands with Umar and taking a seat next to him at the table. It was good to see a familiar face in the unacquainted Japanese restaurant.

Umar sat down, too. "It's been a few years," he said, "but I've heard some good things about you in the meantime, Ishmil. You have a wife now and a few kids?"

"Yes. I have a beautiful wife and three children, alhumdullah. I've been working a lot, that's why I haven't been around. Traveling everywhere you'd possibly imagine. I'd been in Egypt for three years. My father has a few friends that hired me to help setup their businesses. My wife and I figured we'd get more use out of my expensive accounting degree working overseas. Plus, the thought of raising children in an Islamic country was a big seller."

"How was that experience?"

"It wasn't perfect. But I do appreciate having the privilege of my children being surrounded by Muslims. I have to admit I'm glad to be back in the states." He smirked. "When I got the phone call from Tara that you're interested in joining the family I had to rush over here to escort her to dinner. I haven't seen you in such a long time but I know nothing but good about you and your family. I saw this coming a long time ago."

"Speaking of Tara, where is she? I thought you two were going to show up together."

He chuckled. "You know how women are; she's in the bathroom somewhere fixing herself up. I'm going to tell you this, Umar, she's excited to be here."

Umar bit down on his lip to suppress his smile. "I wasn't quite sure how she'd felt about my inquiry. Her reaction was kind of bland."

"Masha Allah, she's very excited. Tara even told me she cannot wait to sit down with you to make sure you are sure about her, because if I approve of you and she agrees then hey you're part of the family, man"

Umar nearly reached out to shake Ishmil's hand and walk away dancing to wedding bells. He had it out for Tara for so long, and just as Ishmil had nothing but good to say about Umar's family, he too only had honorable things to say about them as well. Together, they'd make a powerful, well blended Muslim family with a lot of knowledge and education to pass down to the next generation. It would be everything he'd been taught to do as a young man; secure a good wife that will give your children good names and teach them the deen. Their union would be everything his relationship with Celine couldn't offer.

"Are you sure she's ready to get married so soon? She did just get out of a divorce."

"Truthfully, I worried about that but Tara's a big girl, and for some reason she's able to move on from her feelings extremely well. She's interested, that's a good start. You don't have to get married tomorrow or even a few months from now. Take a few months to get to know her and make sure you're interested as well. We all have skeletons in our closet. That's my sister, but like you said I've been gone for a few years."

Umar agreed. He definitely had a skeleton in his closet that he needed to hide but he was sure after he and Tara grew to know each other a little more Tara would fully understand the situation that he was in and forgive him. Tara was one of the popular babysitters at the mosque growing up. Besides, she loved children.

"I'm going to sit over there." Ishmil pointed to a hibachi bar where a chef flipped the spatula high into the air, then clashed the utensil onto the grill while slicing and dicing away. "I trust you. I know you're not going to do anything disrespectful to my sister. If you need me however, I'll be sitting at the bar drinking my club soda and enjoying tempura vegetables."

Tara walked over to the table and pulled out a chair before Umar had a chance to stand up. She was gorgeous in a maroon butterfly abaya, lots of gold jewelry and a shiny gold hijab wrapped in a manner that not only displayed talent, but also patience and care. He loved women that took the time to detail their appearance. Umar being the flashy brother he was, admired a woman that knew how to dress and put an outfit together without having to take everything off to do so. Tara was classy.

Ishmil winked at Umar before patting Tara on her narrow shoulder and walking off. She sat silently, worrying Umar that he'd ruined his first impression. Then again, he and Tara had known each other for years, there was no need to be nervous. He did however, want to assure her that he was a gentleman and the right guy to be by her side.

"As salaamu alaikum," Tara finally said, as she gave him a brief wave and a smile that girlishly lit her eyes up.

"Wa alaikum as salaam. Masha Allah, you look amazing, sister. Please don't take my compliment as any form of disrespect."

"Umar, you don't have to be so formal."

"I understand, but I want to give you the same type of treatment I would give a sister I didn't know."

"Well," she said, "technically it's been so long since we've seen each other you really don't know me."

"I can agree with that."

"But since we're adding compliments to tonight's menu, I would also like to say that you look amazing as well."

Umar was dressed in his favorite crisp white thobe accentuated with black cuffs. He made sure his barber cut his hair hours before. His beard was lined sharply with a razor making it even neater and apparent than usual.

A waiter came to their table, took their order, made a few horrible jokes and then she walked away. Everything seemed to be going well, so far. He even allowed Tara to pick his meal. Sushi was not his thing, but for her, he decided not to complain and to give it a try.

"May I ask what made you want to go to a sushi restaurant?"

"It was something I picked up while in California. We went to a lot of nice Japanese restaurants. There were a lot of sushi eateries. I guess I've missed the opportunity to enjoy a night out and Japanese."

"I've never been much of a sushi guy, more of a cheese steak and chicken wings man," he laughed, "but I decided to give it a try just for you."

She smiled slyly. "Is there anything else that you would like to give a try just for me, Umar?"

Umar didn't know how to react to the question. She was flirting and being a little aggressive, and he liked it. Tara didn't know who she was getting involved with. The way he craved being next to her, she was playing with fire.

"I'm sure there are a few things I can think of, sister," he said and smiled, "but we'll have to save those things for later. Right now I want to figure out where your feelings stand in regards to marriage, and if you plan on having me stay in your life."

Tara stretched the cloth napkin over her lap, smoothing it out as she spoke, "I'm in a good place, alhumdullah."

"I am, too," he said. "My career seems to really be taking off. This would be the perfect time for me to settle down to find a wife and make sure I'm praising Allah to the fullest."

"I'm surprised to hear that. For most men, whenever their careers are taking off they usually define that to be the worst time for them to settle down and get married."

"I can't agree with that. When your career becomes the forefront of your life usually Allah and practicing Islam comes second. The thought of having a good wife that will worship and praise Allah while reminding you of the religion should be the perfect reminder that you need, in shaa Allah, to keep you grounded."

She looked impressed. "That makes a lot of sense. It seems you have put a lot of thought into this."

"I have," he said.

The waitress delivered the food. Pathetic portions of sushi decorated their plates in a circle with a side of hot tea, and a splash of pasty green stuff that he didn't have the slightest desire to taste. Looking at the fickle amount of food and considering the hefty price, it had better be worth it. Tara though, looked eager to dive in.

She used her chopsticks to maneuver the food, said bismillah, chewed and swallowed, then continued, "What is going on with your career now that's so different than the past couple of years? I've been watching you. It seems as though your career hit a big boom a few years ago and you've managed to keep it going, alhumdullah."

It was nice to know that even in California, Tara kept tabs on him. Umar had yet to break the news to anyone about the possibility of moving to Africa, yet, he thought he could confide in Tara. She seemed like the overly supportive woman he would need in his corner. He wanted her to know about SFN now so if they'd decide to be together moving to Africa would obviously be on the table.

"I was offered a position with SFN."

Nearly choking, Tara jerked forward to hear more, eyes bulging. "Oh my gosh, Umar, that's wonderful."

"But I was made an offer for Africa."

"Wow. How did you make that happen?"

"Rashid, my boss, told me they needed a commentator for the continent of Africa. We haven't fully worked out all the details, but it's not a long shot, he's pretty sure I'll get it. I would have to move there possibly in order to have the job. It would call for traveling from country to country."

"Are you really considering doing it?"

"If Allah blessed me with a job that can possibly take my career to the next level and make it easier for me to provide for my family, then of course. I'm going to do whatever it takes. That's what a man does."

She smiled bitterly. "But you can do that here, can't you?"

"Why? Would moving to Africa happen to be a problem for my future wife?

She blushed. "She's going to have to think about that." Tara took a sip of her water before speaking again. "I really don't have an answer for that question, right now. I've always fantasized about living in other countries. In another continent, too, but I never thought it would come true. That's a big move, Umar."

"Yes," he said, "a good one too, in shaa Allah. It could have a ton of Islamic reminders. Living in an Islamic country could be less fitnah."

"Different fitnah," she corrected.

"On top of that," he said, "you would look amazing on the red carpet next to me at events. How would you like to be the wife of a news reporter? Travel to big award shows and sporting events? You'd be right by my side dressed in the finest designers Africa has to offer. Beautiful luxurious gowns to match my suits; you wouldn't have to work. You could just stay by my side."

She scowled. "I'm not giving up my job, Umar, no matter who I marry."

That sounded bizarre.

"Why wouldn't you? If I'm making enough money to support our family why would you waste time and energy working every day when you can just focus on important matters."

"Like?"

"Like the home and making sure that everyone in the family is doing right by Allah."

She leaned back. "Because I have my own dreams. A part of the problem when I was in California was that I wasn't allowed to pursue them."

Finally, the good stuff.

"Was that why you two got a divorce?"

"Partially," she said.

"And what would make the other part, Tara?"

"My ex-husband had dreams of his own and for his family. The dream that he wanted to live in I just couldn't provide or be a part of."

"Well," Umar said, thinking about her reaction to his dream of working in Africa, "that seems kind of selfish."

"On whose behalf?"

"I'm not quite sure."

She didn't seem to like that answer. Tara's hands were placed in her lap, flattening the already straight napkin with her eyes down in her lap. "There's nothing selfish about a woman being realistic about the fact she cannot provide something a man wants."

"No, there's nothing selfish about honesty. In all actuality, honesty is the least selfish thing that you could give in a relationship." He was reminding himself more than he was reminding Tara.

She looked up. "Then how could you say I was being selfish?"

"I'm not saying you were being selfish. I just said that I'm not sure who was being selfish with the ordeal. Maybe you were being a little selfish by not being flexible, and maybe he was being selfish by not being flexible as well."

"We tried to compromise."

"Would I be wrong if I said I'm glad you didn't succeed?"

Tara relaxed her posture which was very defensive and smiled, leaning closely to Umar, she said, "Would I be wrong if I also said I'm glad?"

"Do you still talk to him?"

"This is our first sit down. I would rather not talk about him or to him, at all."

She was right. It was best to drop the subject. They'd spent enough time discussing her past marriage. It was more important to talk about their future. After they'd both enjoyed their so-called meal, two shots of warm tea and a long conversation about all the plans they both had for the future, Tara and Umar were glad to know they were pretty much on the same page with life. There was only one thing that Umar had to ask before they proceeded any further. He wiped his mouth and gulped down the rest of his tea, and said, "Before we go any further with pursuing this, I have to ask you a question."

"Yes?"

"How do you feel about children?"

Out of nowhere, Tara looked rather uncomfortable. Her eyes shifted away from Umar's face and then went blank. This wasn't good at all.

"I like children," she said flatly. "You should know this already."

"I do remember you being one of the babysitters that the masjid."

She nodded tersely. "I enjoy the thought of having children and it seems as if one day I would love to have some of my own."

Another plus on her board.

"I know we're not supposed to talk about the past, but you and your husband never had children. Was there a reason for that?"

"Like you said," her words went back to being free of emotion, "I'd rather not talk about the past."

"That's fair enough." He lied. "You answered my question. I understand."

Umar was not satisfied with her vague answer and refusal to discuss anything about her ex-husband or the life she left behind in California. He still wanted to figure out any information he could about the woman she'd become. Everyone changed after a divorce. She was doing a good job at shielding those changes.

"Have you been on a lot of sit downs?"

"Oh no," she said shaking her head, "Not since I've been back in Philadelphia. And you know how Ishmil is. He's not going to allow just anyone to take my time."

"So I should be flattered?"

"You should feel pretty confident. You've been sitting here for the past hour and a half and I haven't walked out of the restaurant yet is an excellent stamp of approval."

They both laughed.

"That's good to hear. I'm pretty sure if I told you I had three children you would probably bolt out of the door, anyway. Ya now, being that you don't have any."

"You have three children?"

"No, I don't have any children, yet. I'm assuming because you don't have any children you wouldn't bother with a man that did."

"I don't know if it would bother me. I like children. I also know parenting can be really hard. It would take a lot of patience and a lot of love on my end, but I think I have a little to spare."

Umar felt a rush of warmth fill his heart. "Well that's nice to know. Most people aren't open to the whole step-parenting thing."

"At first I wasn't. The older I get the more I realize it is a big possibility. If I had children of my own and needed to remarry I would want someone to love them as
well."

"That sounds fair."

Umar heard all he needed to hear. Tara was okay with being a stepparent and he was sure once she fell madly for him over the next few weeks she wouldn't have a problem with being his wife. Not only that, but after further discussing his offer at SFN, she kind of loved the idea of living in Africa. Tara even considered compromising with giving up her nursing job to be a full time mother and wife. From what Umar could tell Tara was very flexible. He also liked that even though she carried herself fashionably she wasn't a very materialistic woman. Tara seemed to be patient and very understanding. Umar could also tell she had a wild side he was looking forward to exploring. He was going to give their relationship a few more months but Umar already knew it was only going to be a matter of time before he'd have to break the news about Celine. The moment he did, he was also going to propose to Tara with a stunning ring. Women loved jewelry. Platinum made situations hard to disagree on. After the ring was given plus whatever she asked for her dowry, she'd certainly give him the go and move to Africa.

Umar just had to finish getting all of his ducks in a row with Celine before he left the country. There was no way he wouldn't be there for his first born's birth. Celine. Umar still wasn't sure how or when he was going to break the news to Celine, but if she was going to pack up and move around the world then he would allow her to do so, too. If not–life and co-parenting, went on.

C10

The obnoxious shrill ring of Celine's cell phone startled her awake. She picked up the device and leered at the screen. Her mother. It was 6AM–even earlier in Toronto. There wasn't a reason in the world Celine could think of to cause her mother to call so early. Frustrated and rightfully annoyed, she contemplated answering. Whatever her mother needed to discuss could wait until the afternoon. If someone was sick or injured there was absolutely nothing Celine could do. Not only was she far away, but she was broke. Outside of the debt she had to Bella–which she honestly didn't intend to pay, Celine didn't have a coin to splurge. So if her mother had intentions of hustling a few dollars from her to help with bills back in Toronto, as plenty of times in the past, she'd be better off playing scratch-offs than phoning Celine.

She groaned, it *was* her mother. Celine snatched the cell phone from underneath the pink and leopard comforter, and slid her finger over the screen to answer.

"Good morning." Celine's voice was straight to the point and that of a croak.

"You're not up yet?" Her mother's questioning with an accusing tone made Celine recall her childhood. She was so pushy. Maly, Celine's mother, seemed to have a passion for being bossy; although, Celine only had faint memories of her mother even being an employee. Boss? Yeah right!

Celine sucked her teeth and tisk'd. "I don't have to work today, mother."

"And why not? I hope you didn't lose your job, Celine. You have to be more responsible. Is there a holiday today? Are you sick?"

"Asking if I was sick should've been your first question," she said, "not implying I'm irresponsible or that I've lost my job."

"I just want you to have a good work ethic, Celine. I'm a concerned mother."

She had some nerve! Maly was the type of woman that talked the talk but never walked the walk. Celine always hoped she wouldn't inherit that trait.

"You don't have to be concerned I am working very hard. I just needed a day to myself." Celine, more irritable than she was when she'd first answered the phone, hesitantly pressed forward with the conversation. "If you thought I had to work then why are you calling so early?"

"I wanted to remind you Nathan's birthday is next week."

"And?" Celine wore a quizzical frown she'd wished her mother could witness first hand. Not that the thought of her little brother's eleventh birthday ruffled her nerves, but it was what she knew her mother was hinting at that caused the instant increase of friction between them.

"And," her mother snippily countered, "he would love for his big sister to buy him something special."

She knew it was coming.

"Well sorry, Nathan, right now is not the time."

"Celine don't be so selfish."

"I'm not."

"You are. I worked awfully hard to support you and your excursion. You just had to go to school so far away. How many times did you ask me for assistance?"

Never!

"Mom, I just don't know what kind of help you're expecting."

"He wants one of those new Xboxes. Ya know, the video game system?"

"I know what it is."

"Well?"

"You're his mother not me. I can't afford to send the kids money for their wants every time a birthday arrives. Maybe when I'm paid again I can send a pair of sneakers, but Nathan won't receive a four-hundred dollar game system."

"Hmph." Maly's snickering attitude really made Celine want to end the call without another word.

"How much do you have towards it, mom?"

"Celine, I have a ton of bills and your little brothers and sisters to care for. I don't have any money to make your little brother's dreams come true. Sorry if that makes me such a horrible mother. I didn't realize the same person that throws money at rich designers just to wear one of their overly-priced handbags was the same young woman that won't spend the same amount of money on one of her siblings. I should've known the little girl from Toronto that wore hand-me-downs and was pleased with shopping at thrift stores was now too hot to trot. Too good for her own family."

Maly loved making Celine feel guilty. Yes, Celine loved shopping and expensive items, but she worked for them. It wasn't her job to care for her little brothers and sisters. Due to Maly deciding to have so many children and being left to parent alone Celine never experienced name brand shopping until she left for the states. She hated being teased in school for being the pretty girl with the homeless child's look. Maly may not have been one-hundred percent to blame–Celine's nowhere-to-be-found father took a large portion of it; however, Maly's unwillingness to work didn't help. Celine refused to be anything like her mother. She wanted more for herself and her child.

"I'm not too good for my family. I love you guys. I just have a bit of a situation that won't allow me to help buy the gift. Not right now, anyways."

"I will let Nathan know."

It was a selfish ploy on her mother's behalf to make her feel bad. Yet, Celine did. A twinge of guilt poked at her heart. She really didn't want her little brothers and sisters to endure the same childhood she had filled with birthdays and Christmas's full of letdowns.

"Mom," Celine said, "I really don't have the money, but as soon as I do I will help, I promise."

"Thank you, Celine. I knew you were the same girl I raised. You always did have a heart of gold."

Celine seethed with disgust. Maly was an excellent manipulator; too good to not put it to productive use, actually. Had she'd been a sales woman of some sort Maly probably would've been the head hancho of her company in no time.

"Mom, I'm really tired. I promise to call you in a few days and Nathan on his birthday. Tell everyone I said hi."

"I certainly will, Celine. Do you plan on visiting us this summer?"

No.

"I'll try to make arrangements. Contributing to a video game system for my little brother kind of takes away from my travel fund."

"So you say," she snickered. "I don't think you like us very much, Celine. You haven't visited in a year. Canada is not far from Philadelphia. I'm sure you could travel more often."

Celine released and disgruntled sigh and bit down on her lip in efforts to shield her vicious tongue. Her mother was poking and tempting an argument too early in the morning.

"I will do my best to travel home or help out in whichever manner is needed."

"Good."

Seemingly satisfied with Celine's answer, Maly ended the conversation without a measly goodbye. Ugh! Her mother was so rude and needy. Celine could never do enough or be around enough to please her mother. If only Celine could give her mother a piece of her mind she would've, but what good would that have done? Maly only heard Celine clearly when Celine was agreeing to one of her absurd requests. Outside of that–Maly just didn't care.

Celine lifted the blanket, swung her legs over the bed, and stepped into her cozy, pink feathered slippers. The sun was already high and beaming through her apartment window. Soon, it would be a sweltering ninety degrees in the city–something she had yet to get used to. Actually, the spring heat wasn't so bad; Celine was just in an extremely cranky mood. Between her mother, jailing, and being ignored by her baby daddy; Celine's anxieties couldn't bare intense weather. Baby dad! That word was catastrophic. She wouldn't dare allow the degrading term to slip from her lips. The silent thought alone was enough to make her shriek and quiver with anguish.

Since Celine had acquired a little free time with her call-out she decided to use the time productively. Not feeling too positive about being capable of holding down a complete breakfast, she opted for a banana and coconut smoothie and settled at her laptop. Her fashion and gossip blog could use a few updates, and she hadn't gotten a chance to post the pictures and review of the Yellow Lace club premiere. So after powering her computer and Photo-Shopping the pictures to a respectable lighting, Celine got to work on her website.

Within an hour the blog was complete and published. She rated the club five stars; it had an undeniable ambiance that promised her return after the baby was born, of course. The drinks were excellent, DJ had the perfect selection, and the owners managed to have a packed house. Plus some famous socialites were there to party as well. Celine was definitely glad she didn't miss out on such a lavish and popular event.

After trolling around the internet surveying several websites which featured baby and parenting tips, as well as a few with healthy eating tips, Celine stumbled across a site she'd never heard of: Drama Mamas. The name seemed befitting for the blonde-haired woman on the site's landing page with a pregnant belly and a malicious glare painted across her very pretty face. She looked like drama, and was definitely a mama. Celine laughed. Is this what her life had come to? Either way, the site looked fairly interesting and at least useful for a good laugh.

The site proved to be more than fairly interesting; it was a hysterical outlet for soon-to-be mothers to unleash their dramatic woes, and to look for advice on how to handle their ungrateful

counterparts. There was even an article titled Craddle Robbin';
encouraging women to get the most bang for your buck in the
nine months prior to delivery. It was rather intriguing. But there
was another article that caught Celine's eye.

As if highlighted in gold italics, the words Social Media
Secret, popped out of the screen. She clicked on the post.
Leaning in desperately longing for an answer to her desire to
flaunt her happiness, Celine ogled the laptop. The detailed and
very juicy piece discussed the unfair treatment that men show
their child's mother on social media during her pregnancy. It
mentioned how for nine months a man will not mention a
possible baby until the day of birth, and how it was an injustice
to the mother. She agreed. The article also mentioned why it was
so important as not only a mother, but as the mother of the child
to make your presence known. Tag him in pictures and create
conversation around him. "Your baby should not be a secret and
neither should you," the article commanded.

Yes! Yes! Yes! Celine couldn't agree more. She didn't
deserve to be ignored or a secret. Umar needed to man up. For
the next nine months Celine intended to be a key player in his
life and the star of the show. She'd make sure of it—starting
tonight.

C11

In support of Muslim Night with the 76ers AME offered their staff free event tickets, plus one. That was a big help. When Bella and Celine exited the ramp of the Expressway highway, the line towards the Wells Fargo Center was filled with bumper to bumper traffic. The city's great Muslim community came out to support the event in very large numbers. Knowing there was a large Muslim population in Philadelphia was one thing, but seeing the support and people clumped together at one time was another. She didn't want to undermine the event or disrespect the community, but she did however, want to make her needs clear to Umar.

A little less than thirty minutes later, Bella drove into the parking lot and found a space way in the back. It was the best she could do considering the parking available. Swerving the car into a tight space, thanks to the jerk that wasn't mindful of the parking lines, Bella entered the spot and turned off the engine.

"Listen," Celine said, just before Bella opened the car door. "Let me handle everything."

"What does that mean?"

"I know you've had a few drinks—"

"I haven't."

"Bella, stop. I can clearly smell wine. I'm not chastising just advising. I would hate for you to make a bad impression. You can never be too sure who will attend the

event."

Bella nodded her head. She was a fashion student and in the beginning phases of her modeling career. The amount of buying power and potential prominent figures that may have been in attendance was very high. Allowing a loose tongue due to a few drinks to ruin her career was a no-go. Celine wouldn't allow that.

"I understand, Celine. I'm just here to support you, that's all. I hate how Umar is ignoring you and treating you so harshly."

"Me too," Celine muttered, than opened the car door.

She tried not to sound so sullen but it really did hurt. Celine would've never guessed Umar would behave in the manner he had. He was always so pleasant to be around; which was why she had a crush on Umar the moment she landed eyes on him. He was well put together from head to toe. The brunette curls adorned on the top of his head were trimmed neatly and looked soft to the touch. His beard, although she was never a fan, made him look manly and gave him an edge. It was obvious he worked out, and Umar was also very popular. She liked that about him. Being that Celine wasn't a well-known person until she left for college, and even there she struggled with her identity, she enjoyed entertaining the dream of being on the arm of a person so many loved. Above all of those wonderful things, Umar was extremely humble and down to earth. He wasn't loud and offensive like most of the reputable men she knew. Umar was mild-toned, witty, and very encouraging. He motivated her tremendously to give everything at AME her best. Umar always found a way to lace regular conversation with Arabic phrases and different pieces of the Quran, and Celine liked that as well. She'd never met a man that was religious, yet hot. Not to mention, Umar always smelled amazing. She wasn't sure what scent he wore, but the smell was extremely enticing.

The two women hurried across the parking lot, stood in line, and finally entered the building. Instantly Celine felt out of place. She didn't bother to ask Bella how she'd felt. The arena was packed with men and women; some dressed in standard American styled clothing, and others draped in Islamic garments. All of the women were covered in some fashion, from what Celine could see anyways. Feeling slightly embarrassed for arriving in a peach, floor-length chiffon halter dress that showcased her protruding upper rack, Celine gripped Bella's hand and made a beeline towards their section.

AME provided spectacular seats for their company. The lower level seating was only a few rows from the floor, just close enough to reach out to the players as they exited the locker room. She and Bella trotted down the cement steps until they reached their seats. Bella shuffled down the row to her seat, bypassing the guests already comfortably seated in their chairs. Some frowned and huffed as she squeezed in the tight area with their faces contorted as if Bella was such a nuisance. The game hadn't even started yet, they needed to relax. Then again, it could've been Bella's not-so-conservative outfit that was the true problem. For it to be an Islamic event Bella stepped out of the house in her finest club wear. Celine didn't find Bella's hot pink cropped belly shirt and black leggings to be offensive, but by the squinting eyes leering through slits from the women with niqabs tied over their faces–her clothing may have offended many.

Celine scanned the court for Umar. He was supposed to do a pre-game and after interview. Unsure if the pre-game interview would take place in the locker room, she waited at the end of the row in hopes she'd spot him among the heap of sports correspondents.

Ah ha! Umar was across the court slapping hands with Kareem Khatab, a very well-known player for the team, engaged in what appeared to be a humorous conversation. They both looked great. Kareem was tall, dark and handsome with biceps built like bricks, and Umar looked equally handsome in a white kufi and white linen pants with a matching v-neck shirt. Just a few feet away was a woman that Celine was unfamiliar with.

She couldn't make out her features completely due to the distance, but Celine couldn't recall Umar ever mentioning having a sister. The woman was cloaked in an African print high-waist skirt composed of yellow, blue and black patterns, a black blouse, and a royal blue scarf. The outfit was nice. Muslimah stylish–she'd guessed, but it didn't compare to Celine's ensemble. Still, she needed a closer look. The woman was a few feet away yet she was stationed close enough to be associated with their conversation. Maybe she was Kareem's wife? Not sure. There was something about how she was closer to Umar than Kareem, and the noticeable way she'd turn her head away whenever Kareem spoke as opposed to Umar that made Celine's senses tingle.

Hmmm, interesting! She didn't like what she was seeing, nor was Celine pleased with the intense amount of jealousy she felt swarming in her gut. There was only one way to settle those insecure feelings. Celine made a bee-line to the steps, straight down to the swinging door attached to the bottom level's barrier, and tapped the security guard on the shoulder with a dazzling smile fixed to her face.

"Yes?" The broad shouldered, dirty-blonde haired, guard said without making eye contact.

"I need to speak with my boss. I'm trying to get his attention but he can't see me, and my press pass is in my bag, which is in the sky box that our company has, but I rushed out to remind him that we need to get Mr. Khatab to agree to show up to our feed the homeless event next Sunday."

The man's emerald eyes shifted to the side and eyed Celine skeptically.

"We need as much support as we can receive."

The guard turned to face Celine and gave her a better once over. She could tell he was forcing back his smile. A half smirk was fidgeting its way onto his face the longer he stared at her.

"Celine," she flirtatiously said with an extended hand.

The man shook her hand, making sure to caress it as he held the hand with a firm grip.

"I don't trust you," he said.

She laughed. "I wouldn't either."

"Are you single?"

"Very."

He nodded. "Would you mind going out to dinner?"

"Hmmm, I don't usually take phone numbers on the job, but I'll make an exception for you."

"Well?"

As if her memory was suddenly struck, Celine snapped her fingers and tisk'd. "My phone is in my bag," she said.

"Mine too," he huffed. "How about we meet after the game?"

"I think that would be great," she lied, "or I can get my phone as soon as I'm done?"

"That's even better, um–"

"Celine," she said, showing all of her sparkling teeth.

"Yes, Celine, that's it. By the way I'm Ra—"

"Rashid!" Celine called, cutting the hopeful guard off mid-sentence. She'd almost missed him stepping out from the locker room pathway and onto the court.

Rashid looked over at Celine and strolled to where she was standing.

"You made me a promise, remember?" Celine asked, referring to the agreement they'd made a few weeks prior in regards to him introducing Celine to Kareem Khatab in exchange for working extra unpaid hours one day.

"Excuse me," Rashid said to the guard, "she's okay."

The guard stepped to the side and opened the door for Celine. "So I'll talk to you later?"

Celine brushed past him with a contorted frown. Not later—heck not ever! He wasn't her type and she had a baby on the way. She didn't even feel the need to acknowledge his silly question.

"So I see you're feeling better?" Rashid stupidly asked as they walked across the court.

"Yes, Rashid, something suddenly crept in me and made me sick."

"A stomach virus?"

"That's what it sounds like, huh?" Celine snickered.

"That's what it sounds like to me," he said.

Celine released an exasperated breath and shrugged. "Where's Umar?"

Rashid looked downwardly over his shoulder with a suspicious glare at Celine. "Why are you concerned about Umar?"

"Because he owes me money, and since I missed a few days at AME this week I need to remind him to go to the ATM before he leaves here."

"Umar *owes you* money, Celine?" He released an annoying chuckle that had he'd not been Celine's boss she would've given him a piece of her mind. "That doesn't sound like Umar."

That doesn't sound like Umar Hmph! what did he know? After seeing Umar turn over a new leaf in the past week, the thought of just how straight and narrow everyone thought he was made her stomach churn.

"Are you suggesting I'm lying?"

"I would never suggest a thing."

Whatever.

"I just said that doesn't sound like the Umar I know."

Celine smiled. "I believe you," she said.

The moment she and Rashid approached Umar, Kareem, and the mystery woman Umar's eyes popped with an unsuspecting flare. Celine grimaced. As handsome as he was, she would not let that sway her plans. He needed to learn a lesson from Drama Mama, she was not a secret!

"As salaamu alaikum, Kareem, this is one of the best interns we have at AME, Celine. I promised her a picture in exchange for a few extra hours. Do you think you can make that happen for me?"

"Wa alaikum salaam, of course." Surprisingly, Kareem seemed humble and not how Celine imagined a basketball player.

Although she could hear his reply, Celine's daggers were focused on Umar.

"I have to handle a few things but I'm sure you guys can handle the picture without me."

"We sure can," Celine said. "I left my phone in my bag, do you mind, honey?"

She smirked and waited for Umar to respond. Totally indifferent to the word honey, Umar reached into his pocket and removed his phone without acknowledging Celine's pet name. She then moved just close enough to be foot-to-foot with Kareem Khatab and posed.

Celine eyed the woman shadily; she too was indifferent towards Celine. Redirecting her gaze Celine smiled at the camera as Umar raised the phone into the air for the picture and snapped.

"Can I see?"

Umar handed Celine the phone. Cute picture. Celine held the phone out for the woman.

"Can you take a picture of my boyfriend and I, please?"

The woman's eyes narrowed quizzically and shifted to Umar then back to Celine.

Celine grinned. "Come one, baby."

Umar's dumbfounded, stunned expression was worth a million bucks–make that two million! He sluggishly stepped next to Celine with a rigid visage. With her lips poked out and her eyes wide, Celine posed and waited for the woman to take the picture.

She did.

Celine took the phone back and gawked at the screen. "We look so cute!" she shrieked. "Thanks—"

"Tara," the woman replied coldly.

"Tara," she giddily repeated, "nice name."

"Thanks."

Celine turned to Umar. "I'm going to send these to my phone and talk to you later, okay? You're doing a great job I'm so proud of you."

Umar forged a tight-lipped smile.

"Thanks again, Tara, these turned out great. Make sure you follow me on Instagram at Celine's Cuisine" she said, "no underscores."

Tara nodded. Celine didn't know who Tara was to Umar, but she would soon have a clue who he was to Celine.

"Bye," Celine sang and turned on her heels, dashing back to the stands.

All kind of thoughts ran through Celine's head as she rolled her eyes at the desperate security guard that found the need to harass her once again about her phone number, and found her way back to Bella. Was Tara really a woman that Umar was interested in? He *could* have another wife. Did that mean Celine's chances of being with Umar was going to be divided between her and that covered up crow? Okay she wasn't a crow, but Celine didn't like her. She didn't like what she saw and she didn't know how she should feel about it.

"Where's my bag?" she hissed at Bella as she lowered herself onto the hard plastic chair.

"What's your problem?" Bella handed Celine her pocketbook.

Ignoring her question, Celine whipped her phone out of her handbag and swiped directly to her Instagram app. After uploading the picture and making sure to add the perfect filter to brighten Umar's face so it was clear to all of her ten-thousand followers she captioned: Me and the Mr. #WeLookAmazing #PowerCouple #MoretoCome #MrBigStuff

She didn't tag Umar. This was for her fans, not his. However, she knew that word would get back to him and she couldn't wait for him to get the memo.

C12

"That's not my girlfriend, Tara, you should know me better than to think I'd have a girlfriend," Umar growled into the phone through a strained jaw.

"Not according to her or any of her ten-thousand followers," she spat.

"Followers, Tara? You're a grown woman concerned about followers. Are you kidding me?"

"Nice way to spin it around, Umar. If you'd just be honest—"

"Now you're calling me a liar?"

"I don't know what you are."

Umar could feel every muscle in his body cramp from the mound of tension building in his body. Tara's refusal to accept his explanation was decreasing his patience with her. It was dwindling down to dangerous levels. He wasn't lying—Celine wasn't his girlfriend, and Tara needed to be a good-forgiving woman and just listen.

Umar thought carefully about his words before proceeding. Her new tell-it-like-it-is personality wasn't doing much for their budding relationship.

"Tara," he said coolly, "Celine is not my girlfriend. There's more to the story, I can admit, but that's not it."

"So what's the story, Umar?"

Umar pivoted sideways and looked to his brother Khalid who was stretched across his bed watching the Youtube interview of Umar and Kareem Khatab on an Ipad. Since the initial upload the video mustered a few thousand views in a matter of hours. Between Kareem's celebrity and Celine's pesky fans reposting her new man's accomplishment, Umar's name was buzzing around social media. People wanted to know who he was. Somehow in the short amount of time, he and Celine had been pegged a new power couple by her blog followers. If only they'd known the truth.

He turned his sight away from Khalid. He was starting to frustrate him by constantly replaying the video. "There isn't a story."

"You just said there was a story."

"There isn't a story I need to tell you, not now anyways."

Umar looked back at Khalid with a pinched expression. Khalid was smiling, in his own world, unmindful to he and Tara's ongoing dispute. The least he could've done was given Umar his damn privacy.

"Ahk, I'm not sure what kind of games you're playing but leave me out of them."

"Tara–"

"No." The statement was cold and straight to the point. Umar felt the razor-sharp word stab his heart.

He'd lost his opportunity with Tara, again. This time he'd have to accept the loss and move on.

"You're absolutely right, Tara, I need to leave you out of this game she's playing."

"So what is the story?"

"I don't want to talk about it. You said you wanted to be out of it so stay out of it."

She gasped. "You're mad at me, Umar? I haven't done anything wrong. You said Celine is playing a game but you're the one that won't tell me the truth about your relationship."

"If you don't want to stick around you don't have to."

"What? This is unfair. If I don't want to aid your storytelling I have to get out of the picture? You play very dirty."

Suddenly feeling overpowered by anger and the reality of his one night stand continuing to demolish his life plans, Umar rushed towards Khalid, snatched the Ipad from his hands, and pointed at the bedroom's exit.

"If you don't want to stick around why should I tell you anything?" He barked into the phone. His tightened glare however, was fixated on Khalid.

They were having a stare down.

"I asked you to believe me and you don't." He pointed at the door, again. "I said I will tell you when I'm ready, why don't you just listen?"

Khalid finally got the hint.

"Excuse me?" she said. "You sought me for marriage."

Umar slid his free hand over his face, venting a tired breath as the hand sluggishly made its way to his chin. As if hit with a moment of clarity; he pushed his lids together and reflected.

"I'm sorry," he said.

"Don't be." Tara was serene with her reply, which only made the knife to his heart corkscrew. "I am not the woman for you, obviously. I won't lay down and listen when you bark submit."

"It's not like that, Tara."

"For your future wife's sake," she said, "I hope not."

The line went dead.

Umar gawked at the crimson End Call notification flashing on the screen of his phone. In shaa Allah he'd clear things up with her when she'd calmed down. He wanted to explain things to her, but first he needed to figure out where he and Celine stood. She was right, it wasn't fair to her.

Like clockwork, as soon as the phone flopped onto the mattress the apartment's intercom buzzed. He could hear Khalid in the living room walk to the intercom and ask who it was. Amplified with energy, Celine spoke her name with a proud deportment that made Umar tremor.

C13

"Just give Tara some time and she'll come around. She'll at least give you the chance to be heard. Then you'll have to tell her the truth about Celine and make dua."

With her eyes narrowed with focus, Celine's fingertips and right ear were pressed against the apartment's door. Considering the pricey cost of the luxury apartment building, the sound proofing of the building was practically non-existent. Umar could be heard discussing with whom she'd assumed was the brother he always spoke of, about that meddling woman from the basketball game. Celine knew Tara was in some way associated with Umar. Now, she had the feeling her power move of posting a picture of she and Umar was exactly what the doctor ordered to push her or any other sister out the way. Celine pressed her ear a little harder to the door with a mischievous grin. Thanks Drama Mama!

"You're right," she'd heard Umar say, "if not, Allahu alim. Besides, with Celine's behavior Tara probably wouldn't have stuck around long anyway."

Celine pursed her lips and flicked her eyes to the ceiling.

"Do you want me to leave? I know you wanted your privacy when talking to Tara."

"No. I think you should stick around. Celine may drive my nerves up the wall." He laughed. "I'll need you to keep me cool."

Celine sneered. He had that right! She'd come fully prepared to drive him crazy–crazy in love with the thought of a family. The fantasy of having the perfectly gorgeous family she'd always dreamed to be a part of as a child had suddenly become very tangible. Celine knew what she'd have to do to make it happen. She knew the exact way to his heart.

Peeling her stiffened frame away from the door, Celine stabbed the doorbell. Not much time passed before the untwisting of locks snapped and the door eased open. Umar, dressed in a black V-neck t-shirt, black basketball shorts, and a pair of flip flops also wore a wavering smile and his eyes sensed he was a little bothered. That damn Tara! No problem, she'd sweep her out of his memory–for good.

"Hey Umar," Celine strode past him and to his brother. "You must be Khalid? It's so nice to finally meet you. Umar speaks so highly of you. You two are blessed to have such a strong relationship."

Khalid puffed out his chest and grinned. "That's me."

"Wonderful," she said, "you're exactly how I pictured you."

Khalid was the spitting image of Umar but with a younger and slightly rounder face. Umar's jaw was chiseled even through his burly beard that could be spotted. Khalid on the other hand had a baby face, perhaps the way Umar looked a few years prior.

Umar closed the door. "Take a seat." He directed Celine with a pointed finger.

Celine did as she was told. Gently scooting onto the hard, red low-quality sofa–which she assumed was purchased at Ikea, she angled one leg over the other and rested her clasped hands on her knee. *Be nice. Be tact. Be supportive.* The brief affirmations served as a means to help Celine guard her tongue and focus on her goals. A trick she learned watching her mother flatter her suitors into the cold, manipulative palm of her hands.

"Celine–"

She raised a hand into the air. "Please, let me apologize before you utter another word. You have an obligation to your community and I totally disregarded and most importantly disrespected it. Not until I realized how many people would view, share, and like the picture did I understand just how much I embarrassed you."

Umar gave a soft head nod and moved closer to the sofa. Celine looked downward at her lap with her lips puckered and her brows pulled in. She sighed.

"You warned me," she said, then slowly lifted her head and met eyes with Umar.

His firm stance was now lowering into a chair. Fist to chin, Umar rested his elbow on the arm of the chair and stared at Celine. He began tapping his knuckles against his chin. She'd confused him. Celine smiled.

"I don't know what to say," Umar said, cutting the silence in the room.

"You don't have to say anything. I shouldn't have done what I did. We need to focus on what is best for our family." Celine drew in a deep breath and released. "Showcasing our sins to a bunch of strangers won't do much for our family or our careers."

"Well, you're right about that."

"Of course I am, Umar." Celine slid to the edge of the seat and paused. "Is it okay if I come closer?"

Umar shrugged.

Celine sunk to the tan carpeted floor and scooted to where Umar was seated. Now, she sat cross-legged in front of him instantly shrinking her to an easier level for Umar to communicate with; a trick she learned on the Drama Mama blog. The article pointed out that often times to effectively communicate with a man you must shrink yourself before him to remind him of his role. It sounded like a bunch of crap, but seeing how Umar's body shifted in a manner that made him look more empowered the moment she sat before him, Celine deemed it as partially true.

"I'll be honest with you, Umar, that woman made me extremely jealous."

Umar raised a brow. "Who?"

"The sister you were with. I'm not sure of her name but–"

"How do you know if she was with me, Celine?"

"I don't. However, I wasn't jealous because she was there with you."

"Oh,"

Celine cupped her hand over her mouth as if embarrassed about what she was about to say. She softly shook her head then dropped her hand.

"Do you want me to be honest?

"Of course."

Celine looked over her shoulder then back to Umar. Umar's gaze shifted upward and he looked at Khalid.

"Brother, can we have a little privacy?"

"You're confusing me, Umar, but sure." Khalid stood and walked down the hallway.

Celine waited for the sound of the bedroom door to close before continuing.

"I was jealous of how beautiful the sister looked. I mean–she looked amazing. I never thought that a woman could be so gorgeous while being covered from head to toe. It definitely pulled at my own insecurities and misconceptions."

"Wow, Celine, I didn't expect to hear that. She was beautiful, huh?"

Her lips parted to spew a nasty interjection but then she remembered; *be nice, be tact, be supportive.*

"Very. She certainly gave me the courage to try something new."

Umar's cheeks brightened. "Something like what?"

"Well," she drew out the word melodically, "I know that if we're going to at least give our child a fair shot in this world we need to do what's best for all of us."

"I'm listening."

"Remember the article I wrote a few months back about why Islam states that the child should take the religion of the father and the benefits I learned as a non-Muslim woman?"

"Yes?"

"I would be a fool to pretend as if I'm unaware why it's so important. This is our child, Umar. I'm willing to give anything a shot for her protection."

Umar chuckled. "Her?"

"In shaa Allah," Celine gleefully countered.

"You're learning, I see."

"Like I said, Umar, I am willing to give anything a try."

He nodded.

"I'll need to study and learn a lot more, of course."

"Indeed," he said and relaxed into the chair.

"Today just served as a wholesome reminder; it's our duty to protect our child. I want to make an honest commitment to learning about what you love so that I can maybe one day learn to love it as well. Our little girl will be covered one day, if nothing else, I need to respect it."

"Celine you're amazing me right now. I never thought I'd hear you say such a thing."

"More surprises are to come." Celine batted her lashes and grinned. "Not to mention," she said, "our family needs a fair shot just as your parents gave to you and Khalid. I didn't grow up in such a loving, well-balanced environment. It would be indecent of us to not commit to being a family when we're perfectly capable of offering such. *We* deserve it."

Umar's eyes were pointed at the ceiling as his fingers danced around his curls. She had him! Goodbye Tara.

"I don't want you coming into Islam for me, Celine, let's get that clear. Anything you do must be for the sake of Allah and your own benefit."

"I understand and agree. I would never convert for a man, which is exactly why I said I need to learn and if nothing else respect it."

"I like the sound of that."

Celine's posture perked as she tilted her head to the side and offered a lingering touch on his leg. To her surprise he didn't even flinch at her touch.

"Umar?"

"Yes, Celine?"

"Can we at least say that we're working towards marriage? I don't know how else to present my pregnancy to my friends and family."

Biting down on his sexy bottom lip, at first Umar was non-responsive. Inside, Celine's body temperature was rising. She knew if he was so infatuated with Tara marriage wouldn't have been a question. Celine was the one carrying his child–the question should've been a no brainer!

"Yes," he confirmed flatly.

Celine stood and jumped onto his lap, swaddling him with a tight embrace. At that very moment Umar's cell phone announced that Tara was calling. He swiftly removed the phone from his pocket and ended the call. Calmly, yet ever so firmly, Celine enveloped her hands around the hand which he gripped the phone and leered at Umar sternly, and said, "I'd suggest you tell your friend you're getting married."

C14

Passing by Celine's cubicle as she trolled on the internet ogling at a Target registry she'd been dedicated to building the past week, Umar quickened his pace and made his way to Rashid's office. He and Celine had been getting along fine. Still, he wasn't feeling the idea of her being so close to him. Not after the stunt she pulled on Instagram. Plus, he had the inkling that Celine had ulterior motives when it came to her sudden desire to learn about his religion. He shouldn't have been so skeptical, he knew it wasn't fair. Regardless of her new catalog of books and constant questioning, Umar's gut told him that something wasn't right.

There was also the honest truth of the matter–he didn't love Celine. Yeah, he wanted to offer their child the best option for the future, two loving in-home parents that is; but he questioned if Celine had to be the one he was home with. Tara was still on his mind, and his heart. The opportunity to love her properly had been a long time coming. Being a family with her in Africa would make a great story for their grandchildren one day, in shaa Allah. Their timing was always horrible. Trying to convince himself that what had passed him would've never hit him, and what hit him would've never passed–such as he learned from the infamous hadith, was becoming harder to accept. He prayed for his marriage to be what was best for him, no matter who it was. Now, he was simply waiting to see who would be the woman he'd marry.

Marriage was one thing. What he didn't want was Celine popping up at his desk, spreading his business, and ultimately making it harder for him to progress; especially with the deal still on the table to take the overseas position with SFN. That was just what he wanted to talk to Rashid about.

The door to the office was cracked open. Rashid was busy with a phone call, cackling and leaned back into his chair with a flattered smile adorned on his face. No doubt he was talking to his wife. For being an extremely busy man, Rashid always found time to cater to his woman. He held up a finger at Umar to give him a minute, gave the salaams and ended the call, then greeted Umar.

Umar closed the door, moved to a chair and collapsed into it. "I have a few things to talk to you about, boss man."

Rashid's neck leaned forward. "I've been waiting for you to have a talk with me. I'd figured you'd come in your own time." His hard gaze instantly made Umar restlessly fiddle with his clothing. He hated disappointing his number one supporter, but it wouldn't be long before the cat was out the bag.

"Celine and I–"

"Are a couple?"

"Are having a baby."

"No, ahki," Rashid said, forcing his eyes shut while dropping his head.

"You're the first person I've told, besides Khalid."

"Umar–"

"I know," he said, "I messed up."

"Brother," Rashid raised his head with a pained expression, "messed up isn't the word. Do you know what our sponsors will say about you? This is a bad reflection on the company. They won't want a representative at Islamic events who has a baby on the way with a non-Muslim woman, and you're not married to her? I don't know what to say."

Umar almost choked on the lump in this throat. "Mabrook? Masha Allah?"

"Na'am, mabrook, Umar. You know congratulation is in order." He gave a bitter smile. "I just don't know what this means for your future with the company."

"I came to confide in you, Rashid."

"You are." Rashid sat straight. "However you're still an employee."

"So what does that mean?"

"That means some decisions have to be made in regards to your position here."

Umar's eyes widened with a blank stare. "You're supposed to be my manager."

"I am."

"So manage this," he said, voice elevated a few notches. Umar stood.

"Control your temper, Umar, just hear me out. If you want to snag the SFN job we need to act now with full force."

Umar was at loss for words. Did Rashid not just hear what he said? Now was not the time to consider going overseas.

"Rashid, I just said I have a baby on the way."

"What I heard you say was that you still want a job and a stable source of income."

Umar headed towards the door. He needed to regain his composure.

"So what did you think would be the solution? At least if you go overseas you'll have a great job and a way to provide for the child, because I'll tell you this, Umar, once this hits the fan you're going to have to either marry Celine or your days at AME will be numbered."

Umar paused and pivoted. "Are you serious?"

"What options do we have here? Your reputation as well as mine and AME's is on the line. I warned you about this, Umar. Now I'm your friend so I'm going to make sure you're on a winning team. The team however, may not be AME."

Umar could feel his jaw tighten as he forced a heap of insults back down his throat.

"Do you understand how much time I've spent helping to build the reputation of this company, Rashid?"

Rashid nodded with cold eyes. "And in one night you destroyed it."

With those words, a huge weight dropped on Umar's chest. He dragged his feet back to the chair and flopped down. Hunched over, face buried in his hands, Umar drew in a tired breath.

"I came in here to ask you if you could transfer Celine to another cite? Just until we get married?" he said.

"So you guys are getting married?"

Umar shook his head and confirmed.

"I'll see if my friend Ben has room at his company for a new reporter. If so she'll love the pay raise and the opportunity to write about fashion and such. Just get this all squared away before my investors find out. If not, overseas may be the best career option. It would still be a winning situation. I know you weren't planning on making a decision so soon, but Allah knows best."

"I'll do what's best for me," he muttered.

"In shaa Allah."

Umar rose to his feet and sauntered back to the door. Just as he was exiting he heard Rashid say, "And please, Umar, make sure she doesn't post anymore pictures. I'd hate for your time here to end prematurely."

C15

Celine rifled through the collection of baby bottles in Target, making sure to read the benefits listed on each box before moving onto the next. Her baby should've been sucking milk out of a gold-gemmed nipple. Until the day her fickle salary increased heftily enough for her to afford her taste in clothing as well as her runway baby, Celine would have to settle for something fairly cheaper. Avent or Latch? Not that she had to make a decision right away; she was only two months into the pregnancy, Celine just found frolicking through the baby isle and witnessing the pinched expression on Umar's face to be a great source of entertainment. Rotating her head just a tad to catch of glimpse of Umar, arms clutched to his chest, with his lips pursed as Khalid seemingly yapped his head off about something she was sure wasn't worth responding to, she laughed to herself. Umar would get over it sooner or later.

She was actually enjoying the frustration he evoked when she wasted time pedaling through stores doing baby window shopping. The day when he finally accepted his new lifestyle, with an open heart, would be the day she'd truly internally amuse his ongoing persuasion of her becoming a Muslim. Until that day, or at least until the day when it was time to actually purchase baby items, she'd torture him with trips to baby-land just as Drama Mama suggested.

"Umar, honey, can you come here for a second, please?"

Although Umar dragged his feet to where Celine was occupied, the way his eyes widened and glowed showed his eagerness to dismiss himself from Khalid's chattering. Goodness! He seemed to always be around these days. Anytime Celine came to Umar's apartment Khalid was there. He was even around when they weren't in the apartment. She knew what the religion said about having a third party around to avoid whispers of shaytan, and all that good stuff, but sheesh! She couldn't even seduce her child's father, better yet fiancé, the way a woman would like to; which to her unbelief was exactly what Umar wanted. No sex until they were officially married. Ridiculous!

"Those are nice," Umar said.

Celine shifted her weight to one side with her head cocked and winced. "You don't even know what you're looking at. Please don't be so uninvolved with making sure our first child has everything it needs to be a healthy and happy bundle of joy," she said, and held the two boxes of bottles side by side, at eye level for Umar. "Now which do you like?"

"How am I supposed to know, Celine?"

She huffed. "Read the label, Umar."

Rolling his eyes and releasing his arms from over his chest, Umar took the two boxes from Celine's hands and gawked at the detailed lists on the front.

"Latch looks nice," he said coolly.

Celine returned the boxes to her eye level. Latch it would be. Honestly, neither of them had the slightest clue about picking out baby items so whatever he gave his input on would have to be the chosen piece. As long as he was involved, Celine was happy.

"As salaamu alaikum," she heard from a distance. Then Celine heard Khalid give an overly-friendly reply.

Snapping her head in the direction of the conversation, Celine leered at the woman who greeted Khalid. The navy headscarf hung in a manner that covered a large portion of her side profile however, Celine recognized the voice and the perfectly shaped frame from the basketball game. Tara wore a considerably loose navy and lime striped garment, but it hadn't managed to hide the fact that underneath she had a killer body. Celine was seething with jealousy. The lousy woman wouldn't disappear. She was becoming a reoccurring issue.

"Small city," Celine said loud enough to break up the conversation between Tara and Khalid and gain a glance from Tara.

Tara turned to face Celine and Umar. Her lips parted as if she was suddenly loss for words gaping at Celine and Umar in the baby aisle cradling boxes of bottles.

She sucked in a small amount of air before speaking. "It is," Tara said, "a very small city."

"Umar," Celine said, nudging him with her elbow, "aren't you going to greet your friend?"

They both starred at each other.

As if she was clueless to the awkward tension between their circle, Celine went on with her banter. "He can be so weird, ya know? I'm sure you do." Celine took a step closer to Umar and smiled at Tara. "How have you been since the basketball game?"

Face tight and shoulders squared, Tara cleared her throat and managed to muster the fakest, most forced grin a woman could give. On the inside, Celine pictured herself stomping Tara's self-esteem all over Targets shiny, tiled floor; however, Celine kept the facade that she was sincerely interested in Tara's tired life.

"Things have been great," Tara said. "I just started a new nursing job."

"Nursing? That is wonderful. I may need you to be by my side shortly." Celine chuckled, alone.

"Oh? Do you plan to be in the hospital anytime soon?"

Damn right! Tara was mocking her but Celine welcomed it. Umar was the only one bothered by the announcement of their child. She wished she could've smeared it all over Tara's beautiful face.

Waving the boxes as she spoke, Celine looked up at Umar who had his body uncomfortably angled away from her like he was preparing himself for a head start to dash away from the two women. "I'm going to put these back. We don't have a need for them right now." She waited for a response but his dumbfounded gaze was focused on his Nikes. Celine leaned towards Tara and said with a hushed tenor, "I'll let you two talk."

Moving to the end of the aisle she pretended to be tuned into the now meaningless baby items on the shelf. Picking up various options of pacifiers and bibs, Celine kept her eyes glued to the articles while her ears were zeroed in on Umar and Tara's conversation.

"Are you expecting anything?" Tara's voice was faint and shaky, but Celine could still hear her disappointed words.

"Now isn't the time to talk, Tara."

"Why didn't you tell me?"

"I didn't have the chance."

"How so, Umar?"

"Tara—"

"You lied to me about being in a relationship."

"I wanted to be married, Tara."

"Well, aren't you getting married?"

Umar paused for a moment. Squinting her side-ward gaze to see what the heck he needed to pause the conversation for, Celine hastily peered back at the items.

"I wanted to marry you, Tara, and you know that," he whispered.

Hearing his admittance made Celine cringe.

"That will never happen," she spit back in a course whisper.

"You don't know what may happen, Tara."

"What I do know is I believed you and I will never trust you again."

That was all Celine needed to hear, and it was exactly what she was hoping Umar would understand, get the freaking hint, and move on with his life so they could finally have the perfect relationship she was sure she could give him. Yes, Celine knew he had feelings for Tara, but so what? Once he accepted their marriage would never happen he'd be fine. They had a family to raise. No woman would ever take Celine's place once the baby began to blossom in her belly. She was sure of that. Umar was a good guy with a good heart. His devotion to his beliefs and family would keep the glue to their relationship tight. No matter how much he or Tara wanted to deny it.

"I'm ready to go," Celine shouted. Umar and Tara spaced themselves apart. Their stupid, sullen frowns made Celine want to gag. "It was nice seeing you again, Tara."

Tara waved. "You too."

"By the way," Celine said, "I really love your style. You'll have to give me some pointers as to where to purchase my garments."

Tara just smiled.

Witch.

"As salaamu alaikum," Tara said, more so to Umar than to Khalid and definitely not to Celine.

"Wa alaikum salaam," he replied.

Chin high, Celine waved at Tara until she was well away in the distance. She then turned to Umar. His jittery fingers were jumping around as if they were looking to ring something– perhaps Celine's neck? She laughed out loud. Umar's tight, jaw grimace was sexy.

"See," she said, "I didn't say a word to her about the baby."

C16

Cooing pet names while delicately gliding her fingertips over the smooth pouch, she took in a savoring breath and predicted how big her tummy would appear in just a few short months. Celine's cheeks glowed as she ogled her protruding belly in the dresser's mirror. The growing bulge was just adorable! Originally the thought of a stomach poking through her clothing and possibly earning her a lifetime of stretch marks was viewed with great detest, but now she loved her changing body. Her little one was tucked inside motivating her to fill up her downtime learning everything she needed to learn about being the ideal parent; even if that meant studying Islam to mend the rips in she and Umar's relationship. He didn't trust her. And she had to admit that she earned his lack of trust. If things were going to change, she'd have to make an honest effort at getting on his good side.

Prior to her decision to make an honest effort to investigate what it meant to be a Muslim, Celine thought she'd earn his trust with a barrage of bedroom loving. But that didn't happen. Umar stood firm on his belief that they shouldn't acquire anymore sins by having sex as an unmarried couple. She'd wish he'd tell his family already so they could get the darn thing over with and she'd have to stop pretending to be so patient with the matter. Her pregnancy hormones were driving her desires crazy.

The ding of her work email notification sounded from her cell phone. Pulling the shirt back over her belly, Celine reached one hand behind her back, pressed it against the lower region, and waddled over to the phone on the windowsill. No, she wasn't far enough along to waddle or to have aching back pains. It was just something she made of habit of doing while at work. She may have agreed not to tell anyone *verbally* about their surprise cub, but nowhere in the agreement did she state she wouldn't give physical hints.

An email had arrived from her boss Rashid. She clicked it. Read it. Then she pondered for a moment. Blinking rapidly, Celine scratched her head, and then read the email again. She was receiving a promotion? That was good news. Great news. What wasn't so great was she'd have to switch locations– immediately. Uncontrollably, her lip curled and ticked as she gazed at the email once again. The more she contemplated over the email the faster the baby seemed to swarm butterflies in her gut. Umar had to have had something to do with this.

He and Rashid were good friends. Did he know about the pregnancy? Probably not considering Umar wanted to keep everything so discreet. Then again, where did this sudden full-time, well-paying promotion come from? The offer to work at an entertainment company, non-religious, which was an associate company under the large umbrella that ultimately owned AME through investments, was quite frankly the most awesome news she'd heard in a long time. Yet, an unsettling feeling was in her stomach. Had she really earned the spot? Celine was a great worker. The best if you asked her. She had a style of her own and was very persistent with seeking information. All of the good things a boss could ask for; which was exactly why she questioned Rashid's willingness to give her up to someone else. No, she shouldn't doubt her skills. Still, Celine couldn't help but think this was one of Umar's ploys to hide the reality he was not the man he portrayed himself to be. Secretly, he was making her resent him.

Celine's life was already complicated. The job would help make financial burdens ease her pockets, but she'd have to get adjusted to a new job, new co-workers, and in a few months she'd go on maternity leave. The commute was only another ten minutes downtown, but she hated the idea that Umar would try to do anything within his power to hide their baby. She despised it.

Using her thumb to swipe out of the fishy email, Celine's first instinct was to call Umar and interrogate him until he confessed to displacing her. She was livid. Celine ran her clammy hand over her forehead then returned her shaking hand to the phone. Her body temperature was rising. The awful part was she wasn't even sure why she was becoming so emotionally confused and upset. It wasn't just about Umar or the baby, it was about life. Celine was losing control of her life. Everything had turned into schemes and planning ahead in order to gain control of what she once never thought about losing. Her life was no longer her own. It belonged to Umar, the baby, a new religion and now a new job.

Clutching her stomach, Celine choked on her developing tears. An assortment of emotions bombarded her heart. Umar had schemed and manipulated just as much as she had in the past couple of months. Only she seemed to be the only one who noticed. She hated it. Even more so, she hated how regardless of how Umar treated her, Celine couldn't stop her heart from loving the father of her child. Love that she couldn't identify when it began to develop, but it had. She didn't want to fight with him. This was supposed to be a happy time in her life. The back and forth, sneaky tick for tack moments they'd grown accustomed to had her exhausted.

Umar won. Celine would take the job, stop fighting, and try her best to be the perfect wife and mother he wanted her to be. She simply wanted the dream pregnancy she'd seen growing up on TV; smiles and kisses with tons of supportive family and friends around her rubbing her belly and buying the baby gifts. That's what she wanted. If she continued to make Umar's life a petty hell she'd never get the peace her baby deserved.

Celine sighed.

The only way she'd get what she wanted to was allow him to commit fully to her life. That meant she'd have to stop hiding the truth from her loved ones as well. It was time to tell her mother about her baby and about Umar.

C17

Something wasn't right. The door knob was knocked out of place and cocked on an angle that left it mangled and dangling from the door. The door's frame was splintered and just off its hinge. It wouldn't shut properly, and through the cracked slot Umar could see the flickering of the TV from the bedroom against the pitch black insides of his apartment. Umar had just arrived at the apartment building after a long evening of planning a campaign for AME's annual Walk for Peace. The wreckless job done on the door displayed that of war. *Bismillah*, he whispered to himself, hesitantly pulling the door back just enough to slip inside without making too much noise. Better to be safe than sorry. If the intruder was still inside his apartment he had to be man enough to face his fate.

The house however, wasn't out of order. A few articles of mail had been tossed around, but other than that, Umar couldn't spot a mass destruction of his property. But the TV was flickering. Creeping towards the bedroom, he wiped his sweaty palms on his pants and took a deep breath. He didn't hear any chuckling or even someone chatting on their phone; he couldn't even tell if there was a shadow in the room. All that could be heard was the sound of SFN playing at a low volume.

The closer he moved the more his heart thumped. Bulky knots formed in his stomach within a few short steps of his bedroom. Then something moved. More like shifted. From Umar's view, someone was seated in his round lounge chair. Khalid. Then again, if Khalid was in his room relaxing, why did it look as if the house had been broken into?

"As salaamu alaikum, Khalid?"

He heard a man's groan and then, "Wa alaikum salaam."

It was Khalid.

Umar stepped into the room and grimaced. It was dark as a forest in the room, but that didn't stop the major shiner on Khalid's face from being noticed against the television's light. A mixture of black and plum colored skin shun under Khalid's eye and on his bruised jaw. His lip looked plumper than usual too.

Umar reached for the light switch.

"Keep it off," Khalid barked, but his bruised lip made the order muffled and distorted.

Umar did as he was told, pressed his back against the doorway, tilted his head with his eyes to the ceiling and sucked in a breath through his flaring nostrils.

Umar didn't attempt at bothering to make eye contact in the dark, but the uncomfortable shifting in the chair was loud enough for him to know that Khalid was thinking of something sly to say. He wasn't sure who his brother had become. Whomever, he needed to get out of his house.

"What happened?" Umar said.

"I can explain."

"Start."

Khalid sniffled just before speaking; not from tears, it was a habit he'd formed as a kid; he always sniffled before confessing to something he'd done.

"I owe some people some money," he finally confessed.

"What people, Khalid?"

Khalid scratched his head.

"This guy, Ronnie; I met him at the casino."

"You owe a guy money that you met at the casino? I let you stay here and you're still gambling at the casino?"

"No, not exactly."

Umar clinched his fist. Khalid was playing some sort of game with his vague responses. It was making the muscles twitch in his forearms.

"What people, Khalid?" he repeated, this time with a strained jaw.

"Ronnie has a poker circle at his house. I was doing well. Very well, actually. All I wanted was the money to use for a deposit for a new place to live and three months of rent after that. The semester would've started back up by then and I could use my financial aid to pay for my housing."

Umar cracked his knuckles and inhaled sharply. "How much do you owe him?"

"Six-thousand." He paused. "When I moved here I thought I'd buy a little bit of time to pay him back."

"You knew this before coming here? You owed this guy Ronnie and moved into my home without telling me?"

He didn't respond.

"Khalid?" Umar's voice boomed with authority.

Choking on his words, he mumbled, "I thought I'd have the money by now."

"Ronnie broke into my house?"

"I don't know how he knew where I was staying."

"What if Celine was here?" Umar surprised himself with that question. Celine never crossed his concerns, but the risk of him losing his child because some thug busted through the door and attacked her had his blood pumping through his vessels at a dangerous rate. The twitching in his muscles quickened as he squeezed his fist tighter, he wanted to pound another black eye on Khalid's already damaged face.

"Look," Khalid said, "I'm sorry."

"Sorry?" he snickered.

"If you loan me the money–"

"I'm not loaning you anything, Khalid. I don't even want you in my house. Call ummi and tell them you're coming over there or ask Ronnie for a place to stay while you work off your debt. I'm done."

"Work off my debt? This man broke into the house and attacked me."

"Time to play in the big leagues, Khalid. I can't help you."

Khalid jumped to his feet and in a flash was chest to chest with Umar. He wasn't his little brother anymore. His well-toned shoulders and arms made him more of an opponent for Umar than he'd been a year ago.

"You're going to put me out?" he huffed.

"I don't even know you anymore, Khalid."

"I'm your brother."

"Ya Allah, you put me and my family in danger with your lies and gambling. You're my brother but you're not my responsibility. Go to ummi. I'll be back in three days. Your stuff better be gone and get the landlord to change the locks." Umar turned away.

"Umar," Khalid reached for Umar's arm but Umar replied by powerfully shoving Khalid in the chest, causing him to stagger backwards.

"Don't touch me," Umar snapped.

"Umar, relax."

"Three days," he said, and disappeared from the room, slamming the bedroom door behind him.

C18

She almost didn't answer the phone. For five strenuous minutes the alarming ringtone specifically assigned to Umar pierced Celine's ears and interrupted her sleep. Whatever he wanted would have to wait. Whenever she needed him he was hardly ever available, and at 3AM, she was not willing to be the gracious one out of their relationship. No, Celine wanted to be a jerk just as he'd been. Bad enough Umar had her transferred to a new location, which she'd start in another two weeks, but now he'd thought he had the privilege of antagonizing her sleep. Celine would never get away with calling him at 3AM. Once again jamming her finger against the touch screen to end the call, Celine jostled the aggravating device under one of the many pillows on her bed, and turned over.

"Celine," a voice bellowed from outside. "Celine!" The person called again. And again. And again.

Maddened and full of fret, Celine tossed the comforter back and slid out of bed. Her house slippers would have to wait, she needed to see what fool was outside of her apartment screaming her name at the top of their lungs at this ungodly hour.

Sure enough, it was Umar.

His shirt was stretched, pants wrinkled, and his hair was flat on one side; he looked like he'd been camping on a park bench. Celine frowned. This was just her view from the third floor, surely up close Umar looked worn out and terribly ragged.

"What are you doing?" she yelled down.

Umar raised his stretched out hands in the air, and yelled back, "Can I come up?"

"Ring the buzzer."

A minute later Umar walked into Celine's living room, and she was right, up close he looked beat. His eyes were low, he smelled like a mixture of sweat and air freshener, and his clothes which were always perfectly cloaked on his body looked as if he'd worn them for three days straight. This was not the Umar she knew.

"What happened to you?"

He pushed past her and flopped onto the sofa before answering. "I was sleeping in my car."

"Tonight?"

"Yes,"

"Why?"

Umar kicked off his shoes and rested his back against the sofa. "Is it okay if I lay on the sofa."

She nodded.

Celine moved to the end of the sofa and sat on the edge right next to Umar's feet. She wanted to rub his leg and tell him whatever was bothering him he could talk to her about it, but she held her ground and stayed firm. He hadn't been to her apartment since the night they'd slept together. There were plenty of times she'd asked him to join her to keep her company or to be there to comfort Celine's morning sickness, but he refused. Time and time again Umar had refused to add any level of additional comfort to Celine's pregnancy outside of what he'd thought was right. Now, when obviously in a time of need, he'd ran to her like a wounded puppy.

"My place had been broken into," he started. "The guy that did it beat up Khalid; he has some issues going on right now."

"What kind of issues?"

"I don't feel like going into details, Celine." Umar had the nerve to sound agitated by Celine's questioning. Taking a soothing stream of air in through her nose, Celine placed her hands in her lap and stared downward at the floor. "Why are you always so rude to me?"

"I'm not,"

"You are, Umar. I asked a question, that was all. It seems as if every time I try to get closer to your personal life you have a problem with it."

"His issues have nothing to do with my personal life, Celine. I want to conceal his sins and allow my brother to mask his own flaws. He doesn't need my help to expose him. Can you respect that?"

He had a point. She wanted to know what exactly happened to Khalid to cause someone to rough him up. He always seemed well balanced and like a decent guy. The thought of him being involved in anything that wasn't clean and holy came as a big shocker.

"He doesn't seem like the type to be involved in anything that would cause him to stray from Islam."

"Why do you say that?"

Celine shrugged. "You know, you guys just seem so wholesome."

Umar laughed and lifted his back against the arm rest. "Aren't you pregnant?"

She smirked. "Well, yes but–"

"We're Muslim, Celine, but we're still human. Everyone's jihad is different. Knowing right and implementing it are two different things, get me? He's a believer. Right now Khalid is going through a difficult time in his life. He's changing and is facing the world for the first time. I guess he's finding himself."

"That's a good thing," she said.

"It's a scary thing." Umar was now seated upright with his elbows behind him on the armrest. The original wrinkles in his forehead relaxed giving him a softer and stress-free expression. It felt good to have a sincere moment between the two of them. They hadn't shared a time like this since Celine announced her pregnancy.

"Let me explain this," Umar continued. "Usually we create more fitnah, problems, on ourselves by trying to find ourselves. Yes, we have to go through it and more than likely we can't avoid it, but if it doesn't bring us closer to Allah then there is a major problem."

"You don't think his problems will?"

A serious gaze swept his face. "Allahu alim, Celine, Allah knows best."

She loved when he used Arabic terms. It was exceedingly sexy to hear him put an accent on a foreign language while maintaining his manly-American ruggedness. He was a city boy just as she was a city girl, but Philadelphia was nothing like Toronto. Umar had a lot of wits and street smarts about him that Islam and his polished casing couldn't hide.

"Another thing is that Khalid and I were raised in Islam. It's not like we found our way to it."

"But you told me Allah chooses Muslims not people."

He smiled. "Na'am, this is true. What I mean by that is Islam is a lifestyle that we've known from birth. It's embedded in us. We didn't have to leave the world behind to find out that this was the correct way to live. It's all we know. Oftentimes people take it for granted. Khalid is experiencing things now that you probably learned and experienced a long time ago. The world is fairly new to him. He's like a mouse right now that has access to a field of nuts and berries, but he wants cheese. What he doesn't see is the which cheese smells good and probably even tastes good, is sitting in a warm and comfy house, on a trap."

She sat and thought about that for a moment.

"In shaa Allah he'll be okay. Like I said, Islam is his foundation. Everyone struggles differently. This is my struggle, along with patience and my temper."

"You need to get some rest," she said, standing and passing him one of the sofa's pillows.

"I'm sorry," he blurted.

Celine wasn't expecting an apology. The words knocked her heart so off course she felt her knees giving in as she walked towards the bedroom. With her back turned, she waited for Umar to finish.

"I know I haven't been very good to you. I don't have a solid reason why. I also know that I've said this before and honestly, I'll probably say it again and again. Just be patient with me."

That wasn't the request she'd been hoping for. Celine had been patient with Umar. Too patient if you asked her.

"We all have things to work on." She coldly replied before walking to the hallway closet and retrieving a blanket.

"Take a seat," he said when she returned.

Celine's contorted frown was worth a million words, but she did as he asked and took her place on the sofa. Umar stood in the middle of the living room, angled, facing one of the living room corners. He stood silent. What was worth even more words was what Umar did next. He prayed. A melodic tune poured from his lips as he moved his hands to the front of his shoulders then crossed them over his chest, clasping his wrist with his head low. From motion to motion in various positions of standing, bending, then dropping to the floor and pressing his head to the carpet, Umar transitioned and prayed in Arabic in a manner that she'd never seen him before. His concentration was firm like there wasn't anything in the room but him and his prayer. Celine sat stiff, breathless, observing Umar with adrenaline in her veins. She had no clue what he was saying, but he sounded beautiful and unlike anything she'd heard in church.

Before she knew it he was done.

For a short moment he remained on his knees, toes tucked under, with his hands cupped in front of his face and his back hunched. He whispered something, once again in Arabic, before wiping his hands over his face. Then he took in a heap of air, and then turned to face Celine. He looked refreshed.

"I put our relationship in Allah's hands."

Nervously grinning at Umar, Celine broadened her smile until the fake simper stretched from ear to ear. She wasn't sure if she liked the sound of that. Yes, she believed in God, but Umar needed to man up and make better decisions. She couldn't say that, however. So she said the next best thing, "I want to attend jummuah with you tomorrow."

C19

The darn scarf just wouldn't stay put. No matter how many times Celine shifted, adjusted, and readjusted the pesky piece of fabric, it refused to lay elegantly on her head in the same fashion as all of the other women in the masjid. She couldn't concentrate. The message appeared to be good, although there were unintelligible words and phrases she didn't understand, but she was thoroughly distracted by the scarf and how all of the other sisters in the room, which was filled with women only, seemed to have it all together. They were so poised, cozily seated on their hips with their feet kicked out to the side on the navy carpet fastened with cream and black patterned designs from India–or somewhere foreign. The women looked so holy and in tune with what the Imam was saying. There wasn't the usual hollering and clapping she'd experienced visiting Baptist churches, or the singing during Catholic services; aside from the Imam whom was in the brothers' room, the entire building was silent.

Celine looked up at the forty-eight inch flat screen suspended from the wall that displayed the Imam and the men's side of the room. At first she thought having to watch the service on a television screen from a women's only room was odd–very odd, but it proved to be a sure fire way to make sure no other women were eyeing Umar; like that home wrecking Tara who was perched in the front of the room. She hadn't seen Celine slip into the back; Tara was busy praying along with the rest of the women, but Celine could spot Tara a mile and a half away. She was fed up with running into Tara and her goody-two-shoes persona. Hmph! No woman was that polite and cordial all the time. Her and her phony *as salaam* whatever needed to get married and off of the market quick! Celine's lips curled slyly. Why wasn't she married anyway? Drama Mama *did* instruct its readers to *Dig up Dirt or Get Hurt* in one of their articles. Perhaps it was time to learn about Miss Tara and her disastrous California marriage.

Thirty minutes later the room was cleared out. A few random women greeted Celine with a hug, handshake, or wave, all of which Celine replied with a wary smile; a few women that didn't include Tara, of course.

From the slits formed between the overly-friendly women Celine bobbled her head side to side and observed Tara rush out of the masjid. She'd better not be in a hurry to harass Umar, again. After politely excusing herself, Celine gathered her things and was on Tara's heels.

Tara wasn't in a rush to see Umar. In fact, Umar was nowhere to be found. All of the men were on the other side of the building. Tara, though, was tucked away in the corner that acted as a meeting place between the mosque and the building next door. Back curved facing the street, she was deeply engaged in a conversation.

Celine silently moved in her direction. Tara was rather loud. And not so well mannered as usual. Whomever had her attention had Tara utterly frustrated and upset. It had to be her ex-husband. Tara never appeared in distress or frustrated, she was always delightful and dignified. So hearing an anguished Tara who certainly desired to keep her drama to herself had Celine's brows peeked with inquisitiveness while inching closer to Tara's back. Celine's cheeks glowed wickedly, she was becoming pretty good at snooping.

"Congratulations on your baby, Amin. Alhumdullah, I'm glad to hear you finally have your heir." She sniffled.

Wow! Seems Tara's ex managed to move on quite quickly. Miss goody-good wasn't such a great catch after all. Celine stepped closer. Beauty and brains yet still lame. Umar had no clue she'd saved him from a lifetime of boredom.

"I don't want to move back to California. When you married Melanie it was too hard to handle, but now that she's pregnant," she ran a hand over her eye and sniffled again, "it would be too much for me. To even request such a thing is absurd. You wanted to have a child and Allah has answered your prayers. Masha Allah."

Another wife? This was better than Celine had thought. Tara must've not wanted kids and it sent her husband flying into another woman's arm. Celine tisk'd. Good thing Tara was now aware that Umar had a baby on the way; she'd no longer be a problem once he knew she despised children.

Placing one hand on her belly, Celine reached out her free hand and tapped Tara on the shoulder. "Are you okay?"

Tara glanced over her shoulder and rolled her eyes sharply before looking away. The nerve! Celine was trying to be sympathetic but Tara was too stuck up and ungrateful to appreciate her kindness.

Celine began making circles on her belly and transitioned her pat from Tara's shoulder to her back. Instantly Tara stiffened her posture, glared at Celine, and ended the call.

"Can I help you?" she snipped.

"I just wanted to see if you needed a friend or words of encouragement. You look like you're having a tough time."

Tara gave a silent look and pursed her pouty lips. "I'm okay."

"Are you sure?"

"Yes."

Celine now had both hands resting on her small belly which barely poked out behind the loose shirt Umar coaxed her to wearing.

"Well that's good to hear." She said cheerfully. "I'm off to my doctor's appointment. We're so excited."

"That's nice." Her indifferent tone really bugged Celine. Tara could at least pretend to have an interest in her and Umar's baby. Playing a game all alone wasn't fun at all.

"Do you have any children?"

"No."

Celine frowned. "I'm sorry," she said scooting closer in a hushed voice. "My mother always said not to bring up the topic of children to women of a certain age. It tends to be a sensitive subject."

Tara batted her extensive too-die-for dark lashes, and frowned. "I'm not much older than you, Celine."

"I'm sorry, again," Celine shockingly slapped her hand over her mouth. "My mother also said never to bring up a woman's age. How tacky of me. I really must try to be a better woman."

Tara took a step back and turned to walk away but Celine followed in her steps like an annoying little sister not getting the hint to end the conversation.

"As you see I'm getting used to this covering thing," she said. "At first I didn't get it. But then I convinced myself that if I'm going to win Umar's heart I must be, ya know, submissive and all. What kind of wife will I make if I don't give my man what he wants?"

Tara kept walking.

"A bad one," Celine answered her own question, "and probably divorced."

Tara stopped mid-stride.

"Are you implying anything, Celine?"

"Green."

"Excuse me?"

Celine pointed to the hijab fixed on Tara's head. "The color, green," she said. "It looks good on you. Do you wear it often?"

"I don't know what type of games you're playing but–"

"I'm trying to compliment you, honey, take it and run with it. Sheesh. I always thought Muslim women were too serious, you're just aiding the stereotype."

Tara gasped and held her pointer finger up as she angrily bit down on her bottom lip.

"Masha Allah," she strained the words while trying to sound pleasant.

Oh please! Everyone had buttons that could be pushed. As well as Tara tried to hide hers Celine knew she'd banged on Tara's buzzer.

"I have to meet with Umar," Celine said indifferent to Tara's flustered red cheeks, daggering glare and budding grimace. "But um, in shaa Allah, I will see you next week?"

Tara huffed. "In shaa Allah."

"Good." Celine shrieked and waddled off with an extra sway in her slim hips. Delighted that Tara would be officially out of the picture so she and Umar could move on, Celine began running over various ways to break the news of Tara the baby hater to Tara's EX- admirer.

C20

No one told Celine that her GYN visits would now consist of her womanly parts being massaged and probed like a piece of raw ground beef. She scowled every time the doctor and her aggressive fingers twisted and turned in her cervix just before widening her plum with the dreadfully cold, plastic duck-lipped utensil. Male doctors tended to be gentler. Unfortunately, Umar insisted she switch to a female GYN. To him, it was improper for a man to have that much access to her body unless under an extreme situation where he had to perform to save her life. Other than that, no woman in his life would be fondled by a male physician of any sort.

Celine scooted her bottom to the end of the table and tried to relax her muscles the best she could, but that was nearly impossible. She looked over at Umar. Seated with one leg crossed over the other, and his face buried in a magazine, he was trying his best not to look at Celine during her examination. It must've been nice! All of the encouraging pats-on-the-back he'd probably receive for merely showing up to doctor visits while she was the one that was made uncomfortable and treated like a lab experiment. Seven more months of torture? This was insane.

And to think being held as a hostage for three long hours in a chilling and too-quiet for comfort waiting room, forced to finger through magazine after mind-numbing magazine, just to have a fifteen minute visit with the savage gynecologist was just a warm up for the big delivery; Celine's mind was made up—no more children!

The doctor withdrew the tool, rolled the small stool over to the computer and typed a few notes. Who knows what about Celine's canal was worth documenting. Nevertheless, Celine kept her mouth shut and fixed the paper gown, and patiently waited to hear the news, if there was anything to hear at all.

The doctor smiled. "Everything looks good so far, Celine. You should schedule your ultra-sound appointment." The doctor was a rail-thin, Indian woman with a long black ponytail, and enough eye wrinkles to resemble the driest desert. She may have been a well-paid doctor, however, when she smiled there were evident traces of her underprivileged childhood. The bottom row of her stained teeth, although there weren't any gaps, leaned left and right crowding on top of each other.

"That's good to hear," Celine said.

"Is there anything particular we should do to ensure the baby's health?" Umar said from the corner of the room.

We? That was surprising to hear. Celine beamed a bleak smile at Umar.

"Eat healthy and make sure she's taking her vitamins, for now. If anything changes I'll make sure to let you know."

We both nodded.

"I need to get some paperwork for you two. Feel free to change while I'm gone."

The doctor rose from the stool and exited the room. Without hesitation, Umar turned to face the corner and buried his head back into the magazine. He was so damn weird. Celine and her changing body were nearly invisible to him. She wasn't sure if he was turned off by her or showing what he considered to be respect.

"Hey," she said peeling the paper from underneath her bottom and stepping into her sandals. "I saw your friend Tara at the masjid today."

"Oh really?" He didn't bother to face her direction.

"Yup."

Celine twisted her smile and pulled her white sundress over her head. She'd traded her modest clothing in for a knee-length baby doll dress after jummuah. It was way too hot to not let her skin hang out.

"We had a really brief conversation about my doctor visit. Actually, I was kind of shocked about what she said to me about having kids." Celine hopped back onto the table, her legs dangling as she slowly rocked them side to side.

"What did she say?"

"That she didn't want any."

Umar spun around with his brows quizzically furrowed. "Are you sure about that?"

"Yes, I'm sure, Umar."

"Tara used to babysit the kids during the adult classes. She always had a liking for small children. I'm shocked to hear that."

Chin lifted high, Celine pressed her palms onto the table and leaned back. "That's why her husband married another woman, divorced her, and told her to scram. He wanted children and she didn't."

Umar's smug chuckle meant he questioned her story. "She told you this?"

"Yes,"

"I don't really believe that, Celine."

"Why not?"

Placing the magazine that no longer held his attention on the computer desk, Umar tucked his fists under his arm pits and sneered. "No one knows about Tara's divorce. She's kept it very discreet, as a woman should," he said. "You're telling me out of everyone that has known her for years Tara decided to open up to a complete stranger."

"I'm not a complete stranger, Umar, I'm the woman of the man she's in love with."

"She told you that as well?"

"No, but it's obvious." Celine twirled strands of her hair around her index finger and with a serious deeper tone, said, "Don't think I don't notice for one second the goo-goo eyes you two have every time you run into each other. She's in love with you, Umar."

"I really wish you would move on. Please stop bringing Tara into our situation. She has nothing to do with it."

"So when are we going to get married. You haven't introduced me to your family. The baby is a big secret."

"You need to learn the religion," he said, lacking any interest in her whatsoever.

"I get that, Umar, I do. But learning the religion won't stop the baby from coming or my belly from growing. How much longer do you want us to live in shame?"

Umar's glare shot to the floor. She had him! Celine had finally broken through.

"You said that you're going to keep apologizing and that you're sorry for how you've acted towards us," she said rubbing her belly, "but what has changed?"

"Just a little more time, Celine."

"We don't have any time. Let's get married next month."

"I don't want to marry before Ramadan."

"Why not? Won't it make our relationship a little easier? Plus we'll be able to fast together."

Yeah right, on the inside she was laughing. Celine may not have known much but she did enough research on going thirty days without food and water to know pregnant women did not have to participate.

"Let's start off with you meeting my parents. After that we'll get married."

"I'll believe it when I see it," she snickered.

"What do you want, Celine? I'm giving you what you asked for and you're still not satisfied."

"I want a date not an empty promise."

"Trust me enough to know when I say I'm going to do something I will, okay? Just two months ago we weren't thinking about getting married."

"But if my name was Tara you would've proposed by now."

"You don't know that."

"Sure I do. You're both Muslim, it's understood."

Umar shook his head and stood. "It's time to go," he said.

"That's the truth. I know enough about Islam to know had I been Muslim you wouldn't try to make me a statistic. You would've married me just as you would've done right by Tara and married her."

"Your hormones are going crazy–"

Celine gasped and jumped to her feet as well. "How dare you blame your denial on my hormones, Umar? Just admit it."

"You're not Tara and you're not Muslim. You can't have things you're way that aren't owed to you." He venomously growled the harsh reality sparking tears of hurt, frustration, and acceptance from Celine's eyes. A tear traveled down her check, and then another. Before a puddle fully formed on her face, Umar rushed to Celine, swaddled her in his embrace, and kissed her on the forehead.

"I'm sorry, Celine, honestly."

She shook her head in his chest and tried to pull back but he wouldn't release her.

"Forgive me, please? The doctor will be coming back any minute now I don't want her to see us like this."

"You're concerned about the doctor's feelings?" she sobbed harder.

"No, I didn't mean it like that." He caressed her cheek, wiping away tears. "I suck at this. I'm sorry. You're owed everything any woman would want. You've been nothing but good to me and you really don't deserve anything less but to be honored respectfully. Let me prove it to you."

He kissed her on the cheek.

"We'll go to my family in two weeks. I want to speak with your mom as well. It's time we do things the right way."

She nodded.

"You're beautiful, Celine." For the first time ever Umar rubbed her tummy and smiled. "I should've told you this a while ago, but you look amazing."

Umar had the softest brown eyes and lips that made her body shutter. She gawked at him adoringly. The summer had turned his tan skin the color of hot toffee. As much as she hated him at times, he made her weak.

"I'm not going to pressure you about the religion anymore either, Celine."

"Thank you," she sniffled.

"Allah makes Muslims not people. I won't stop making dua that you grow closer to him, but I will only say in shaa Allah and give it time."

That was a relief. For a moment she felt strangled by the pressure of turning her back on her childhood. There was still hope Umar would accept her for who she was and leave it at that.

"So what now?" she said, pressing her face deeper into his chest.

"Now," he said, "we plan a wedding."

21

"Are you sure you're ready for this?" Khalid questioned referring to the glass case jam-packed with engagement rings ranging from three-hundred dollars to a whomping twenty-grand. It was the first time he and Umar had gotten together since the encounter he had with the guy Ronnie. Umar wasn't interested in Khalid's lofty critical opinion of him marrying Celine–he needed to get his own life straight before offering anyone advice. What Umar was interested in was gaining Khalid's support and making it clear to him Celine would be a part of the family.

"I'm ready," Umar said. "Since I've been staying at Celine's she's turned over a new leaf. We've been getting along great, the same way we got along before she was pregnant." Umar nodded. "I owe this to her."

"Owe is a big word." Khalid frowned.

"She's a good girl. Celine has even taken a real interest in Islam."

"Are you sure about that?"

Umar moved closer to the counter, placing his forearms on the glass to get a better view of the price tags. "Yes."

"How so?"

Umar adjusted his posture and drummed his fingers on the glass. Two thousand was a nice amount to spend on her ring, he guessed. Celine had expensive taste, but from what he could tell the rings in that price range were very nice; something she could wear daily that brought just enough attention without attracting unwanted looks. He waved to the jeweler.

"As salaamu alaikum," Umar called.

The jeweler, who Umar knew was Muslim as well by the painting of the al-Fatiha hanging inside the office, didn't bother to return the salaams. He sauntered over with a crooked smile and bulging belly and a look that said Umar had interrupted the episode of Family Feud he'd been engaged in.

"I said how so, Umar?" Khalid repeated.

Umar heard him the first time but didn't feel like explaining himself to Khalid. This was supposed to be a happy moment. Not to mention a moment for Khalid to make up for the abrupt relocation he'd caused Umar with his drama.

"She's learning tawheed."

"Masha Allah,"

"And she's interested in covering."

"Don't be so naïve, Umar."

Umar twisted his neck towards Khalid, face contorted, ready to chuck words so hurtful his way he'd rethink ever questioning another person's interest in Islam.

"I think you need to be respectful. Alhumdillah she's learning. Celine isn't perfect, but you haven't been around lately."

"I understand that."

"Then work on fixing your own iman."

"You're my brother, Umar, I just wanted to–"

The man sauntered back off. Umar gnawed at the insides of his lip before calling him back over. It was a habit he'd picked up over the last couple of weeks of living with Celine. He was trying his hardest to control his patience before speaking, and thinking three times or not speaking at all.

"As salaamu alaikum, brother, can you please show me this ring?" Although he sounded pleasant, his foot was rapidly pecking at the carpet.

"When I was over there you didn't stop to show me which ring." The man, aggravated in tone, kept his eyes on the game show.

The finger tapping and foot patting stopped. Enclosing his fingers to a fist, Umar huffed and presented a hard smile. "I said as salaamu alaikum, can you please show me the ring?"

"She's not ready, Umar."

"Khalid, now is not the time."

"Wa alaikum salaam, are you finally ready?" the man said.

"Yes," Umar relaxed his palms on the counter, "I was ready the first time."

"No," the man said and stood, "you weren't."

"Umar,"

Snapping around, Umar gave a hard look at Khalid. He just wanted to buy the ring. Between his brother and the rude jeweler, Umar was on pins and needles over something that should've been more like cake and ice cream.

"Listen, I don't know what your problem is with her or why you refuse to accept she's changing but give her the benefit of doubt, Khalid. This is going to be the mother of your niece or nephew, in shaa Allah, just pray that Allah guides her properly."

"Look at this," Khalid said and held out his phone.

He did.

"I love you fisabillah, but I don't want you marrying the wrong kind of woman."

Umar's shoulders circled over his chest as he clutched a clump of hair and sighed.

"Which ring, brother?" the man said.

He licked his lips and pinched his eyes together. Celine was up to her old, childish tricks. The picture Khalid showed him was one she'd posted online no more than twenty minutes ago. With nearly one-hundred likes, the picture of his child's mother, soon-to-be wife, was that of her lying on the bed with her bosoms bursting out of a black-cami top, licking her lips at the camera, with a purple hijab tied around her head and her newly dyed honey-blonde hair peeking out from the sides of the scarf.

This was embarrassing.

To make matters worst, Celine had tagged the pictures #baddieinhijabbi #coveringishot #Muslimandfab

She wasn't even Muslim, yet.

The comments below the disheartening picture only encouraged the foolishness and disrespect towards the purpose of a woman covering. Men and women complimented her on her modesty, or lack thereof. Still, that wasn't the part that made Umar's stomach convulse. From what he could see, the last username to double-tap the picture was AME.

C22

"So you're really a Muslim now, huh, Celine?" Knowing Bella the way she did, Celine pictured her with her brows drew in closely and her face tight with forehead wrinkles.

Celine closed the Drama Mama blog and raised the straw floating in a can of Diet Coke to her lips. "Almost."

"Almost? What does that mean, Celine?"

Rolling her eyes and taking a long sip, Celine uncrossed her thickened legs and stood. "It means that I'm almost there."

"How exactly is one, almost a Muslim, Celine?"

How many times was Bella going to say her name at the end of every self-explanatory question? How else are you almost anything? You're almost there, sheesh.

"I can't explain it," Celine snickered.

"Try."

"I feel like I'm on the phone with my mother and not a good friend that's happy for my life changing in a positive direction, Bella."

Bella blew into the phone. "I am happy for everything that's going in a good direction, Celine-pooh. You have a new job, a new baby, and from the look of it," she elevated her tone, "you and Umar are really doing well."

"Alhumdullah," Celine taunted.

"Huh?"

"It's something I've picked up from my fiancé, Bella. It's saying all praise and thanks due to Allah, giving him credit."

"Oh," she said, "alhumdullah, I guess."

"Very good, Bella, soon you'll almost be a Muslim too."

"I just don't want you to jump head first into anything that you're not quite ready for."

Celine giggled sarcastically and walked through her bedroom, down the hallway and into the living-room. Wincing at Umar's sneaker collection that took up too much space next to her apartment door, she kicked the line-up and pushed them further away. She wasn't too fond of Umar insisting that they'd keep their shoes by the front door and took them off as soon as they entered the house, but she was trying to do things his way, for now.

"What makes you think I'm not ready?"

"Well," Bella dragged out whatever punch she was ready to heave, "I did just see the bizarre picture you posted."

"Bizarre?"

"It was, Celine, to be truthful."

Celine sucked her teeth.

"Muslim women don't dress like that. If you're going to take on the religion at least do it respectfully."

"Oh please," Celine blurted before she had the chance to conceal her thoughts from jumping off her tongue. "What do you know about Islam or Muslims? Last time I checked, there aren't many Muslims in AA meetings."

"That's foul, Celine."

"That is the truth," she said indifferent to the hurt dripping from Bella's words. "Masha Allah. Maybe you need to get closer to God before telling me how to do so."

"It's not like that."

"I'd hope not. You have a long way to go before casting stones over here, Bella-pooh."

Celine had a way of sounding so sweet when she was being such a witch. Sometimes, that's just the way things had to be to keep a friend while making a statement.

She opened her front door and kicked the mail inside.

"Celine, you're right. I'll keep my mouth shut until I have cleared out my own closet. You're doing great and I should be happy for you."

Celine disregarded the bit of jealousy she'd assumed Bella was feeling. She was right. Things were going great for Celine.

"It happens to the best of us," Celine said, picking up a piece of mail that caught her eye. "Let's just work on being the best people we can. Have you thought about your drinking habit anymore?"

"I don't have a habit."

"Well," she said and used a finger to slice open the mail, "please note that after the baby is born I won't be partaking in your drinking binges. I'm a changed woman."

The letter was from the district court.

Celine's eyes jumped around the page looking for the important information. She'd forgotten all about her run-in with the law a few months prior. Really, she'd hoped they'd forgotten about it too.

"I'm happy for your life changes, Celine, honestly."

Bella was unknowingly rubbing the letter in! Not in the mood to tell her friend about her upcoming court date, Celine brashly ended the call. Umar would flip if he found out about this. She wasn't sure how to break the news to him about her felony charge or the fact she could possibly get deported for her bad judgment call.

The door opened. Umar kicked off his shoes with his face screwed with displeasure. Whatever was bugging him would have to wait. She had more important matters to tend to.

"We need to talk," he said.

Celine slid her feet into a pair of house flip-flops, which had her mind not been so wrapped around the impending charges she would've never worn them out of the house, and squeezed past Umar.

"Sorry, I have to go."

She rushed down the hall and across the street to the frozen yogurt shop. Celine wasn't going to map out her plan on an empty stomach. Plus, she needed to be nowhere near Umar when she called home to Canada.

C23

Celine drove the plastic spoon into the strawberry yogurt and scooped a sizeable amount of the soothing dessert, before parking the utensil in her mouth, leaving it to reside there as she thought about the hearing. She didn't like strawberry frozen yogurt. The baby did. Her little dairy guzzler had been craving the frosty sweet treat all day. Seeing Umar barge into the apartment gave her the nudge she needed to head out in the ninety-five degree weather and meet her baby's demand. On her second large cup of yogurt topped with crushed strawberries and caramel sauce–another sweet she never liked to indulge in, Celine navigated through her thoughts of breaking the news of the baby and her possible deportation to her needy mother. Maly expected Celine to be the meal ticket for the family. Celine wished she'd gone back to school herself but Maly still had dreams of being the same glamorous, well taken care of, exotic-Cambodian woman she was before she had her bandwagon of kids.

When she was younger, Celine admired wearing her mother's heels and the way men smiled and talked softly to Maly when they were out in public. They always had the nicest things to say.

That was until however, Celine grew up. Once Celine became a teenager and realized her mother was nothing more than a leech that would rather rely on handouts than securing a future for the children she seemed to pop-out every other year or so, her mother was no longer her hero. Maly was everything she didn't want to be.

Yet, Celine was headed down the same path. Or so she feared. Umar had been making heavy contributions to the household and Celine loved the idea of not returning to work after the baby. Lots of women were housewives, but she felt guilty about loving the idea of becoming one. Maly's constant close-call evictions and inability to provide taught Celine that a career was one of the most important things a woman could have, next to a pair of red pumps.

Celine rhythmically banged her foot against the table's pillar, removed the spoon from her mouth, and using the opposite hand dialed her mother. She wasn't sure how she'd react to the baby, but she needed advice about the deportation. If anyone knew about getting out of trouble, Maly was the most knowledgeable person in her phone to call.

"Celine, my beautiful daughter," Maly sounded unexpectedly ecstatic to hear from Celine.

"Mom, how are you, is everything okay?"

There was loud country music playing in the background and the sound of dishes colliding into one another. A day didn't pass that Maly didn't have a hot meal prepared. Poor or paid, everyone was always fed.

"Everything is wonderful, Celine. I have a new friend coming over that wants to help out around this ragged house I call a home." By new friend she meant a new man.

"That's nice, mom, I'm happy that you're happy."

"Happy is a bit of an overstatement. It's just funny how things work, ya know? I was so worried and upset over your brother's birthday and not receiving the help from his favorite sister to buy him the one gift he'd been asking for for so long, and now look, I meet this wonderful new friend of mine that really took to Nathan. He's like a mentor."

"That's great for Nathan."

"Even better than having a mentor," she was bubbling with excitement, "he offered to buy Nathan the game system."

"Is that why you're cooking?"

"Of course, Celine, the least I could do was offer him a good meal for his generosity."

Celine's features shifted curtly as if her mother could see it. "His wife couldn't prepare that for him."

"Don't be silly. He's not married and even if he was I'd still offer him a wonderful meal for being such a good friend to Nathan."

"A friend to Nathan, huh? Is he Nathan's age?"

Maly exasperated a short sigh. "I'm in a good mood, Celine."

"Okay, okay, he's a good friend to Nathan." Celine took in another spoonful of yogurt. "I have a few things to talk to you about."

"What is it, Celine? I pray you didn't get fired. At first when you decided to move to Philadelphia I worried so much about you making good choices. I follow you on Instagram, ya know?"

Celine frowned. "Do you?"

"Ha, I'd thought you didn't. Too busy posting pictures of yourself with that silly scarf on your head to notice new followers, aye?"

"It's not a silly scarf, mom, it's called a hijab. And anyways, that has nothing to do with me or my job, right now. But I'd forgotten to tell you that I switched companies."

"That's great, Celine."

"More responsibility and for a company that will give me more freedom with my writing." She decided to leave out she'd received a pay increase.

"With more responsibility should come more pay, I hope you didn't forget to remind them about that, hmph."

"That's not what I wanted to talk to you about." It felt like ants were moving around Celine's belly. "Mom, I'm pregnant."

Maly shrieked and dropped the phone. In the background she could hear yelling and screams of joy. This was not the reaction she was expecting to hear from Maly. Nothing of the sort. Perplexed, and feeling the ants in her belly marching even faster in circles, Celine cradled her stomach and waited for Maly to return to the phone.

"Oh Celine, I'm so happy for you."

"You are?"

"Yes."

"Why?"

"Because at one point I was worried you were a lesbian."

"What?"

Maly eased her tone before speaking. "I just wasn't sure. You never mentioned a boyfriend or fiancé of any kind. So I wondered. But now I know you're going to be a mother I'm so excited."

"So you're not upset about me having a child and not married?"

"Upset?" she sucked her teeth. "I was never married to your father and you turned out just fine. Look at you, just beautiful, a college graduate, and independent enough to step out on your own and move to another country."

Celine smiled.

"Now who is the man?"

"His name is Umar–"

"Umar or Omar, Celine?"

"Um…Umar."

Maly hummed. "Did he work at your old job? Is he the reason for you taking pictures in that scarf-jab-thingy?"

Celine drummed her foot harder. "He's not the reason but yes, I did work with him."

"Umm hmmm," she said.

"But he's a good guy, mom."

"I'm sure he is," she snipped. "Going against his morals and religion getting my daughter pregnant, shame on him. Now he's forcing you to wrap up your hair? You're too beautiful to not show it to the world, Celine, remember that. God wouldn't have made you the way you are if he intended for you to hide it."

Celine wasn't sure if she'd agreed with that. From what Umar had been teaching her about modesty, she'd liked the idea of concealing her beauty for the man that deserved it the most and her family. The man that cared, married, and provided for her rather than the countless undeserving men that just wanted to lust and feast their eyes on her womanly figure for their own perverted pleasure.

"He's not making me do anything mom, but thanks for the advice."

"Good. And make sure he's not controlling. I don't like the things I hear about those men. They don't want their women doing anything."

"It's not really the men, it's the guidelines they've been given to be good people." Celine shrugged. "It's really not that bad."

"Bad enough," she said.

"We'll discuss the baby further. There's something else I need to talk to you about now that that's out of the way."

She waited.

"I got into a little trouble and I have to go to court for public drunkenness."

"That's not a big deal."

She obviously didn't understand the extent of trouble Celine was in. Celine dismissed the idea of telling her. It was better to wait until she spoke with a lawyer before alarming anyone.

"You're right, it's not."

"I've done a lot of bad in my time, Celine. But there's always an old Cambodian proverb my grandmother used to tell me that helped me deal with it."

Unsure which of the many unclear phrases she'd spit out from the web of sayings Celine's great-great grandmother would say, her mind switched to picturing the many billboards she'd seen of lawyers on the subway.

"If you know a lot, know enough to make them respect you, if you are stupid, be stupid enough so they can pity you."

Half listening, she glowered. "What does that mean?"

"Figure it out, bye."

"Bye mom," Celine said and pressed the end button.

She wasn't sure if her mother was calling her intelligent or dumb. How in the world that saying applied to her life was beyond Celine. What she did know was it was time for her to return to the apartment. Her stomach couldn't bare another mound of frozen yogurt, and she wanted to find out what Umar needed to talk about.

C24

Umar lectured Celine for about twenty minutes about why the picture of her wearing a hijab and not properly covered was inappropriate. She got it. The hijab was something very meaningful to Muslim women as a reflection of their obedience to Allah. It kept them modest and protected them not only from unwanted attention, but also from them partaking in certain sins since they were constantly reminded of their role as women of God in society. Celine understood that before the sermon and after listening to Umar ramble on-and-on, she was at the same place of understanding as when he first started his Islamic heart-to-heart.

What Celine didn't get was how he didn't have the compassion to allow her to investigate her personal feelings towards the hijab. He did want Celine to become a proper, Muslim woman, right? How else was she supposed to find her Muslimah swagger if she didn't play dress up from time to time? This was going to be a serious change for Celine. One that would require an entirely new wardrobe, exchanging her pumps for flats and other less attractive footwear, and let's not even discuss the issue of nail polish or perfume!

"You're selfish," Celine spat.

Baffled, Umar pushed his shirtless back against the counter, furrowed his brows, and strapped his arms over his chest.

"You are," she said in reply to his fed-up stance, "I'm going through all of these changes for you, Umar, and you don't seem to care. So what? I decided to stage a photo-shoot in hijab, big deal. You should be happy I'm considering wearing it. How many women that are Muslim don't wear their hijab, huh?" she gave him a second to respond. "A lot. So if you ask me, I'm stepping in the right direction. You may even want to consider being proud I've taken an interest in covering all of this hotness just to be your wife."

"You're not doing it for me, Celine."

Celine flicked her lashes with a hard roll of the eyes.

"If you're not doing it for your lord then don't do it at all."

She huffed.

"I want to introduce you to my family, Celine. We can't go much longer without telling them about the baby, and I feel as though I've been wrong by not allowing you to meet them."

She perked up on the inside but on the outside she reeked of disdain. Sure, Celine wanted to meet with his family, but she just knew that Umar would make another outlandish excuse for her not to do so. He always did. Right in the midst of an argument he'd find something–anything to sway her to do things his way in order to get what she ultimately wanted. He was a manipulator.

"I'm ready, Celine."

She raised a brow.

"But you're going to have to come as a proper woman. My mother will have a fit if she sees you dressed, ya know, indecent."

"Indecent?"

"To her standards, that is."

"Well hmph," she said, "I'll just have to be indecent."

"Celine–"

"Enough is enough, Umar. If you wanted a decent woman than that's what you should've gotten pregnant. But you didn't. You wanted to walk on the wild side. You wanted to taste something that you knew wasn't any good for you. No, she's not good but she's fun, is that what it was?"

His smug chuckle zipped raging hormones through her blood and elevated it to dangerous levels.

"You're going off on one of your pregnant tantrums again."

"Don't belittle me, Umar." Celine could hear Maly cheering her on. "You're just trying to control me."

"Control you? Celine, you can't be serious right now."

"I am."

"Me asking you to dress decent is not trying to control you."

"Then what do you call it?"

"I would call it showing my family respect."

"You," she said sharply aiming her finger at him and stabbing it in the air between words, "should've thought about respecting your family before you shamed their prestigious name."

Umar's face drooped with a complex mixture of anger and sadness. She'd hit a soft spot.

"I'm not going to take the burden of shame for you. You're making me pay for your mistakes. Now it's up to me to live a lie just for you and your family."

He walked to the bedroom. As fast as she could Celine made a bee-line to the room and slammed the door behind her.

"Do not walk away from me," she said.

"I'm not arguing with you."

"Since when does a conversation simply end because you're angry?"

He stepped inside the bedroom's bathroom, turned on the water, and washed his hands.

"I'm talking to you, Umar."

"You don't know anything about shame," he said in a somber tone that was hard and cold as a block of ice. "You're father abandoned you and your mother has children with every man she thought she loved. You struggle with your identity because your mother is Cambodian and your father is a deadbeat white man that had had enough of her leeching ways. You're so busy trying not to be like your mother that you're turning into her."

"I can't believe you—" Celine charged into the bathroom and struck Umar on his side, leaving a red blotch on his sandy skin tone.

He didn't flinch. "You needed to hear the truth," he said and washed his face.

She pounded a fist into his back. Then another. He silently took every last one of her punches until he was done washing his feet and turned off the faucet. Celine's eyes were flaming red and freed every tear they'd possessed. She was sick of him. Sick of trying to make something work that just didn't work. It was hard trying to make a man love her. Deep down she knew if it weren't for the baby they'd be nothing more than coworkers that had a fling. Defeated and struggling to pace her breath with the baby fluttering around her belly, Celine took one last haul at Umar's ribs.

"Are you done, now?"

"I'm sick of you," she sobbed.

Umar scooped Celine up and carried her to the bed. Gently laying her down, he cupped his hand over her mouth and held it firmly. Both of their eyes were alert and zeroed into each of each other's. He held his hand there, allowing her teardrops to moisten his flesh until she calmed down.

"I'm going to pray," he said, "you can either sit here and cry or you can go in the other room. But if you attack me while I'm praying, I can't control my reaction."

His stern scowl warned Celine that he was done playing games. She nodded. Umar removed his hand and stepped to the side. Her knees were a little shaky. He kind of scared the crap out of her with this threat. Wiping her tears with the back of her hand, and sucking in a few sniffles of air, Celine calmly stood and exited the room. What type of desperate fool had she become? He had little regard for her feelings. Even in the heat of the moment he refused to cater to her emotions. To soothe her and to tell Celine that he loved her, and they'd find a way to move past their differences was too much to ask. That's all she wanted was certainty. He wouldn't give her that. Umar was too selfish. Just as Maly said, if you're smart then know enough to make them respect you. Whether they were together or not, Umar was going to learn to give her just as much respect as he did to his religion. She too deserved attention, time, and care.

Just as she was walking out of the door to head back to the yogurt shop, Celine caught a glimpse of the letter from the courthouse. Her life was in shambles because of Umar. Ever since she'd let him in her world it had fallen so far down the hill she didn't know where to start to get back to the top. Meanwhile, he was living life in a manner that was insistent on making hers harder. She should just leave. Pack her things and move back to Canada since that seemed like it would be the outcome of her arrest, anyways. That way Umar could go on about his life and she could really be like Maly, since that's how he felt.

That wasn't a bad idea. Celine and her baby could live their life free of the confines of Umar's control and their inability to make good, parental decisions. Her mother would love that. Tomorrow she'd talk to a lawyer and weigh her options.

C25

Being that Celine already had an OB-GYN appointment scheduled, she decided it was the perfect time to stop by a lawyer's office to dig up more information about her case. Clifton Bradshaw, a lawyer Celine stumbled upon in a local newspaper, seemed to be the perfect choice for the matter at hand. Clifton was a swanky man in the ad. She loved his midnight-black slicked down hair, charcoal colored suit, and the blood-red tie draped around his neck. The tie eluded he was dedicated to business. Out for blood. His motto was The Real Man in Black. Celine could only hope he possessed one of those light thingies that would be able to wipe all of her problems away–for good.

Clifton wasn't very professional, though. Celine's wait time was short lived in the shabby little office located on Spring Garden Street. It didn't look much like the office of a hotshot attorney but who was she to judge? She needed help and she needed it now. The small plainly decorated white and grey waiting room harbored just a few plastic chairs, side tables, and an endless supply of Time magazine. Behind an enclave that separated the waiting area from Clifton, his secretary sat typing away on a desktop computer. Other than the college aged secretary dressed in a forty-dollar pant suit, or perhaps something she'd found at the thrift store, there wasn't any sign that Clifton was a real power player, at all. Actually, it appeared more so he really needed business.

Clifton, whose height and build humbled the likes of a basketball player that went into early retirement in his 30's, called to the young woman to allow Celine to step behind the barrier. You would've thought they'd at least use a walkie-talkie or some kind of device to seem more professional. But once again, who was Celine to judge.

Celine sauntered to the counter, swung the latched door open, and walked to Clifton's desk. He stood, shook Celine's hand, then gestured for her to take a seat. She did, and immediately her hands began to moisten and fidget. She couldn't help it. Saliva quickly gathered in her mouth, watering with anticipation about whatever news she was about to receive. Nervous was an understatement. Celine's heart was ready to beat through her chest.

Clifton quietly opened a manila folder filled with a few papers, which she could only assume the documents had information on her upcoming court date. He stared at the folder for a few more seconds, eyes squinting and wrinkling in their corner as if he'd never looked it over before, then returned a softer look to Celine and grinned before glancing back down at the papers. She tried to read his expressions, but Clifton was sending her a mixture of emotions. His concerned smile would transform into a frown, then wiggle side to side from cheek to cheek as if he was swishing mouthwash around his mouth. Every now and then he'd give an a-ha or hum with understanding. All of those intriguing sounds were only making Celine's heart race wilder. And still, he had yet to remove his eyes from the paperwork.

She was going to have to pay this man a whole lot of money to get her out of this problem. She didn't have time or a dime to waste on a useless consultation due to Clifton playing games. Impatiently growing tired of her concerns, Celine slammed her hands on the desk and gave him a look of frustration and disappointment.

Startled, he shot his eyes from the paperwork to Celine's after the bang her hands made on his desk. She glowered. Clifton anxiously closed the folder, leaned back in his chair, and clasped his fingers over his lap.

No longer showing a sign of concern or distress, Clifton took a deep breath before speaking. "This isn't looking too good," he said.

Of course things weren't looking so well, that was exactly why Celine came to him in the first place. As of now he showed no signs of being any help whatsoever. A total waste of time.

"Yes, I know this, Mr. um–"

"Bradshaw," he said proudly.

"Yes," she said with a weedy smile, "Mr. Bradshaw. I understand things aren't looking so great for me, that's why I've come to you. I really need your help to be able to understand what exactly this case entails."

"Typically getting arrested for public drunkenness would not be a big thing but being that you are here on a student visa, and you don't really have citizenship to keep you in this country, this could possibly mean deportation for you, do you understand that?"

"Yes, I do understand."

"Good. Now I can talk to the judge and try to make this matter vanish but the bigger problem is even if we could get you off with probation, it would only be a matter of time before your citizenship would be up for questioning. So the likelihood he'll be forgiving is very slim. We have to make sure to make your character out to be something fantastic. You did say you intern for a religious company when I spoke with you initially, correct, and that it was very important for you to keep the position for your school?"

"I used to, actually. Now I work for an entertainment company but it is still important for me to maintain my internship if I intend on returning for graduate school in the fall."

"Hmm," he said, "we'll have to see what we can do to finagle that. The point is, at the time you were working for a religious company, Muslims at that." He wrinkled his forehead and looked at Celine. "I'm guessing you don't follow the belief system."

"No," she said unsure of what he was poking at.

"That's perfect. Merely working for an organization that doesn't agree with your own religious beliefs shows some sign of good character and willingness to go the extra mile to achieve. A true public disturbance and downright criminal would never do such a thing."

Well, Celine did have an outstanding character, she couldn't disagree with that. Heck, if working at the company was all she needed to show that she was as good of a person as she needed to represent, wait until they got a view of the golden child curled inside her belly.

"You also look like you're carrying something in your belly, aren't you?"

"Yes, sir, I'm three and a half months pregnant."

"Oh excellent, as long as we have a female judge there is no way she would want to send a caring mother away from the father. He is American right?"

Celine nodded yes, not wanting to show her growing irritation with Mr. Bradshaw digging into her personal life. "Sir, he is American."

"Excellent, so that means if you guys get married then you would become an American citizen."

How did that slip her mind? Marrying Umar had a lot more benefits than she'd realized. For the first time since the appointment started Celine felt relaxed. Her problems would be wiped away as soon as she and Umar were married. By married she meant through the courthouse; not just by way of Islam. Umar argued religious marriages were honored by the government but Celine couldn't afford to risk it. All was left to do was to speed up the process.

"Sorry to ask so many questions about your personal life," he must've picked up on Celine's halfhearted answers, "but there is something I have to ask you, it could make the case smooth over a lot better with the judge. Are you and the father in a relationship?"

Fairly ashamed to admit that she and Umar weren't quite in a relationship and the way things were going lately they weren't quite on the path to getting engaged, either, Celine gave Mr. Bradshaw a nod.

"Well, I would only hope a man that has a woman as beautiful as you would be willing to marry you in order to keep you in the country. Do you think he would be willing to do so?"

"There's a possibility. We have been discussing marriage."

"We'll have to work something out for you two. Your court hearing is in just three weeks and if you guys can get a marriage license so we at least have some type of documentation to take down there by then, we could nip this thing in the bud and you could be back to work in no time with your feet up and not a worry in the world. You like the sound of that, don't you?"

"Yes," she couldn't hold back her glee, "I do."

Of course she did. That was the one thing missing right now in Celine's unbalanced life–not having a worry in the world. For the past couple months Celine's life had been going up and down and all sorts of spirals. To think in just a few more weeks if she and Umar were to get married that would not only pick up her problems as far as being a pregnant-unwed mother, it would also end her trials and tribulations with the law. Celine had to seal the deal somehow someway.

Mr. Bradshaw clutched his fist, centering them on the desk before he moved inward, and said, "Miss you know we're going to have to discuss a fee for this? I'm going to have to talk to the judge in a personal fashion which means I may have to slide her some money and I will also have to be paid as well. Are you able to commit to a deposit so I can get started?"

Money–now that issue Celine had yet to figure out; how to pay her way out of trouble. She just didn't have the resources to pay for a lawyer. Asking Maly wasn't an option, or at the very least asking her for a small deposit. Other than her mother and Bella she really didn't have a clue who to ask. Reality burned in her belly, she was going to have to come clean to Umar sooner or later. Most likely, it would be sooner.

Celine was pretty sure when she actually talked to Umar he would support the idea of marriage and hand over the cash. He would do whatever he'd have to do to secure his family in his custody. He may not have been too fond of Celine, but that was just the kind of man he was–a responsible one, overall. Umar was groomed to put his family first.

"How much is it going to cost me to pay you and take care of the judge?"

Jeering a scandalous grin that almost made Celine second guess their business transaction, he said, "My fee is going to be five-thousand, but I'll need at least twelve-hundred dollars to get started, and the balance a week before the court hearing, usually. However, you have less than three weeks to get the payment. Do you think you'll be able to do that? If not, I'm not going to be able to take this case."

Celine huffed. She was not expecting Mr. Bradshaw to request such a large amount of money. There was absolutely no way she'd have the balance in such a short amount of time. Celine never considered she'd have to pay the lawyer in just three weeks. It was the first time she'd ever used an attorney. All over the television were ads stating we don't get paid unless you win, Celine hoped Mr. Bradshaw would be as understanding as the other lawyers.

"I'll get it," she said, because she didn't have a choice.

Celine still had to pay Bella back on top of all of her just-to-get-by barrage bills. It seemed like the money was going faster and faster; just as fast as all of her problems. She could no longer keep up and hold her head above water.

"I'll get the money," Celine repeated more to herself than Mr. Bradshaw.

The shady attorney reached his hand out and took Celine's in his and held it gently as he stood. Celine lifted from the chair as well.

"I look forward to hearing from you soon. I look forward to working with you in the future as well. I'm sure you'll want to use my services if you ever need it."

Celine forged a smile in response.

She hoped Mr. Bradshaw delivered as promised and she wouldn't ever need a lawyer ever again. By the looks of his scandalous grin, Clifton Bradshaw may have already made a deal with the devil and Celine had just signed as a witness.

Celine thought for a moment before she spoke. "What if you don't win Mr. Bradshaw? What if you can't get the judge to let me off easy?"

"Celine," he said indifferently, "I do not make promises when it comes to the law but I will make a promise that I will do my best as long as you do what you have to do. Everyone plays their part. I can't see any judge telling a married, pregnant woman she has to leave the country."

That was good to hear.

For a moment Celine basked in the feeling of having her family together–in America, and knowing all her troubles would soon have a passport of their own and be far-far away. She decided she'd liked Mr. Bradshaw after all; he deserved to gain a little trust just for his efforts, despite his unkempt, tasteless little office.

There wasn't much time. Celine was going to give herself at least another twenty-four hours before talking to Umar. That would give her enough time to concoct a plan to make sure Umar felt urgent to marry her.

C26

Now was not the time for pride. After their scuffle Umar and Celine hadn't spoken in days. He remained in the apartment, on the couch and only coming home during hours when he knew she was away or asleep. Regardless, Celine needed his help and was sure that he would give her exactly what was needed; it was just about doing exactly what Maly said. *If you are dumb then make them pity you*, rang in her head. Celine had her pity party revved for Umar.

The plan was to paint the picture of how his reaction to her announcement of being pregnant hurt and damaged her heart so much she ran to the club hysterically upset where she met some friends to seek advice. Only the best advice Celine's *kufar* friends offered was to guzzle glasses of wine until she saw the bright side of things.

Umar knew Celine wasn't much of a drinker even prior to her conversion-excursion. Explaining to him that through her depression caused by his reaction, of course, she gulped down more glasses of alcohol than usual. Then Celine would go on to detail how she couldn't find her keys and her baby-bladder just couldn't take the pressure, concluding her arrest as one big mix up turned into something extremely bad. Certainly he wouldn't want her to be out of the country. Once she spilled the beans, Umar would do whatever it would take to save their child so they could all reside in the same city.

After she left her appointment Celine thought long and hard about how she could deliver the message to Umar. Dramatic would probably be the best way to go. She thought twice, somber and apologetic would most likely swoon Umar in the manner needed. Celine even thought about hooking up with Khalid. She didn't know what type of dirty business he was involved in, but if it was something was bad enough to piss off Umar, it was probably a good money maker. For the next few hours she worked out her act, and scaled the apartment and every crevice she could think of in hopes of finding any money Umar may have left or misplaced around the house. If possible, Celine would use it for her deposit, that way she would only have to finagle the balance out of him.

As life would have it, the apartment and all of the items Umar kept there were dry.

Umar walked through the door and gave Celine a lifeless hello just as she finished sweeping through the closet and then strolled passed her to the bedroom. This had been his routine for the last couple of days. She hated the way they weren't speaking. Her behavior that day had been insane and intolerable, at the very least, still the silent treatment was more distressing than if he'd hollered and yelled her into shame.

Caught completely off guard by Umar's next move, Celine watched him return from the bedroom towing a large, gold gift bag with a pink bow tied around its strings' handle. This had to have been the first gift he'd ever given Celine. The sudden change of heart was alluring. It was the right time to butter her up and make her feel awful inside. She loved the idea of Umar actually showing a romantic side, but she wished he would've done it days ago. Days before she knew she'd have to ask him for a hefty amount of money to cover her legal expenses.

"I want to apologize for the things I said about your mother," he said then handed over the darling bag, "and you as well. I should've been more sensitive about your situation growing up. That was very hurtful and not something that should be used as a tool to insult you. It's really been bothering me. I'm ashamed as a man to have stooped to that level."

Unsure of what to say, and not wanting to ruin his sincere moment, Celine let him continue before speaking.

"I planned a dinner in three days for us to meet with my parents. I want to introduce you to the family. You're past due to finally become a part of the family. I know how I treated you was unfair. I put a lot of stress on you. I'm ready to show you and the baby off to the world."

She still didn't know what to say. This was not expected, by far. Having Umar apologize when Celine was the one in boiling water only made matters worse. When Celine came to the breaking point of confession, she couldn't even afford to sweeten him with a gift.

"So what's inside the bag?" Was the best thing she could think to say.

"Take a look," he said, and she did. "I understand you don't want to be forced into wearing something you're uncomfortable with, so I bought you something more your speed."

Celine took the bag and removed the piece of clothing inside. It was an elegant hunter green long sleeved maxi dress covered with a khaki colored lace print design. The dress was fitted at the top but had long pleats that started at the mid-section and stopped at the bottom. A baby doll collar matched the hunter color along with the thick cuffs. It was gorgeous. Celine held the dress to her body. The precious ensemble came to an end right below her ankles. It was modest indeed, but not out of Celine's comfort zone. The dress had a very vintage school girl look, classy, yet it was very fashionable–high fashion runway material, in fact.

He hadn't bothered to buy her a hijab to match, which made her even more elated over the gift. Umar was actually compromising. She wanted to compromise her attitude with him as well.

"Do you like it?" Umar asked.

"Actually, Umar, I love it. Is it okay if I give you a hug?"

"Come here." Umar brought her in for a hug and gave her a peck on the forehead. There was no place like being wrapped in his arms. Even through all of the drama, there was no denying that. "You know I have good taste. I'd figured you would like it."

Celine nestled her head against his chest and squeezed him just a bit tighter. "Umar, thank you. I really appreciate your efforts."

Having to tell him about the court date would have to be delayed. The lovely dress made it that much harder for her to admit the flaws she had. Umar was far from perfect but overall he was a good guy and would make a good husband–and a good father. He deserved the truth. Celine, however, couldn't pull herself to do it. Maybe giving Khalid a call wasn't such a bad idea. He was already in deep waters with Umar. Khalid wasn't going to come forward and tell Umar about anything they'd scheme together. That would be the perfect solution. Celine would go to Khalid, figure out how they'd come up with some type of money scheme, and split the pay. Finally being in with the family, Celine was looking forward to joining them at dinner in three days. Getting involved with Khalid would be the best way for them to bridge the gap in their relationship.

C27

"My son tells me he's interested in marrying you" Umar's mother, Zaynab, said dully.

Although she tried her best to fake an inviting conversation with Celine, the long, dry moments of silence in between every five or six pineapple and chicken kabobs she stacked on the bamboo serving tray left no guessing Zaynab was not the least interested in Celine. It was the first time they'd met, Celine really was trying to be a good sport. She understood his mother had to warm up to her. She knew with any first time meeting, parents had to sort out their feelings for the new woman in their son's life. Still, Celine could tell it was much deeper than that. Zaynab allowed her body language to exalt what she attempted to guard with her tongue. His mother made sure to keep her distance at all costs walking around Celine, nose high as the sky and chest puffed with revulsion. It was rude. And Celine was really starting to get fed up.

Celine, after taking in some air and thinking twice about the delivery of her answer, finally spoke. "Yes, we're both interested in marrying each other."

"It was just shocking to hear. I wasn't expecting Umar to propose to a woman anytime soon." She completed the pattern of chicken, onion, pepper, pineapple, and looked up at Celine, shooting yet another disapproving frown. "Especially not a woman that didn't quite meet his standards."

Wow, how vulgar! Celine just couldn't believe what she'd just heard. This from a so-called pious woman? Hmph!

"I'm not quite sure what you mean by standards, Mrs. Talb."

Instead of answering, Zaynab returned her gaze to the kabobs and continued working on the plate.

"You know," Celine said, nibbling on a piece of chicken she'd picked up from the chopped pile. "I'm really really happy to have the pleasure of meeting you all. Umar comes from such a nice background. You have a lovely family. It's all Umar talks about."

"We worked very hard to make sure Umar and his brother had the best."

"I intend on doing the same for my child." Celine slapped a hand over her mouth and dropped the chicken she'd been biting just as she finished her statement.

Screwing her head sideways with the evil glare that only a mother could foster, Zaynab looked at Celine and then returned her eyes back to the kabob. "You should eat the chicken you dropped."

"Excuse me?"

"Oh, you don't know the sunnah so you wouldn't understand," she snipped. "It's proper etiquette."

"I'm not eating chicken that fell on the floor. I'm sorry if it contradicts your beliefs but I am not going to eat something that has floor seasonings."

"You come into my home and don't want to adhere to our customs?"

Zaynab was insane and nothing like Celine imagined a Muslim woman to behave. Eat from the floor? Celine didn't know what part of the religion stated that as proper etiquette but she had it at the top of her list to question Umar.

"I apologize, once again, if I offended you. But you are Muslim, I am not, yet anyways," she made sure to imply as to not rub Zaynab any worse than she already had. "I need to grow in that area."

"You're not Muslim but you want to marry into a Muslim family and not abide by their rules when entering their house? Hmph." His mother was so uncouth Celine wanted to give her a piece of her mind.

"I guess that's where we stand."

Zaynab moved a step away as if terribly bothered by standing within inches of Celine. Her concentration was narrowed on the kabobs, lips pursed, roughly sliding the veggies on the stick.

"When you say child," she fell silent, then said, "are you implying you and Umar are having a child?"

"Oh, I wasn't implying anything. I just stated something I wanted to make clear, as a woman that is."

Zaynab twisted a frown that told Celine she didn't believe a word she'd just said, lifted the plate, and walked off into the dining area.

After sitting and blessing the food, forks clashed against the square, white ceramic plates and glass goblets filled with ice water gently hit the table staging the only noise interruptions during their hushed dinner. The indoor BBQ wasn't much fun. Umar's father occasionally engaged Khalid and Umar in questions, which were followed by short answers by both brothers, and here and there he'd include Celine in his questioning too. Zaynab kept one eye on her plate and one on Celine, and ever so often, darting both of them towards Mr. Talb.

Eating dinner at the Talb's was a lot different from other times she'd been a dinner guest in someone's home. This family was actually a lot different than what she'd ever witnessed. The household didn't contain any alcohol. No one disrupted the meal to step outside to have a smoke. There wasn't even a barrage of inappropriate jokes, arguments, or use of foul language to weave through the dinner. It was rather bland if you asked her. Dinner, which consisted of the kabobs, rice, and a fresh salad, wasn't even accompanied by jazz music or any sort of music for that matter to keep them entertained. It was the most straightforward, basic dinner date Celine had ever partaken in. Eat and stare, that was all.

That was until Zaynab wiped the napkin over her mouth, and said, "If the girl is pregnant then just go ahead and say it, Umar, you don't have to waste our time."

Caught by surprise, Celine looked at him and then back to his mother.

"I didn't think having a nice dinner with the family would be considered wasting time."

"I think we both know why she's here. Celine's already let the cat out the bag. So just go ahead and say it. Own up to your sins."

Umar took a sip of his water before speaking. "With all due respect, Ummi, I don't have to confess to anyone. But as I said, I wanted everyone to meet Celine."

This conversation was not going to go well. Wide-eyed and totally lost for words, Celine sat back, took a chunky bite out of a kabob and watched the verbal slip-up she'd made a half hour earlier in the kitchen unravel. This time, she'd allowed Umar to take full control of the situation. Typically she was not a step-back-and-let-a-man-take-hold of anything type of woman, but in this case she'd have to make an exception.

Umar's frustration was visibly surfacing, his features hard and directed at his mother although in tone he remained even tempered. "Celine," he didn't make eye contact as he spoke to her, "please don't allow this incident to make you mad. It's a shock for her to find out you're almost part of the family."

"I am NOT being rude," his mother interjected. "The young woman decided to blurt she's carrying a child without formally introducing herself or her family's name."

Mr. Talb looked at Celine in a sad way that made her feel guiltier than Umar had ever managed, then looked back to his wife.

"Mom, she's pregnant and I'm owning up to my responsibilities by marrying her. Just as you taught me to do for my future family and just as abu did for Khalid and I."

"As we taught you to do?" his mother said with a pinch of disbelief.

That's when his father and his mother silenced immediately and looked away from Celine, Umar, and Khalid whom managed to sit unnoticed throughout the entire debacle.

"Her problem is not with you, Celine," his father said, "please don't be confused or hurt."

Celine didn't respond either way.

"The problem is that Umar knows how hard his mother and I have worked to make sure he did things properly."

"Until this point have I disappointed you?"

"No, actually until now you made us very proud; this just so happens to be one of the greatest disappointments you could give us."

"We have given you your rights as our child," his mother said. "We tried our best to instill in you the importance of doing things correctly. You're more than old enough to decide what is best for you and your future family. You won't have rights over the child that you are bringing into this world."

Umar's glare eased and looked down at his plate.

"You want to get married now, alhumdullah, that is the right thing to do, Umar, but that does not change how we feel. Give us time. I'd hope you didn't come tonight expecting for us to give you a party over this ordeal?"

Celine was puzzled over all this talk about rights. They were disappointed with Umar, which was understandable, but he was twenty-six years old and completely independent from them-for Pete's sake it was just a baby. She was glad Maly wasn't so uptight.

Umar thought for a moment before speaking. "You're right I did not do my job to give my child its rights, and you are also right I shouldn't have gotten Celine pregnant without being married. Will you deny that it is the qdar of Allah?"

"The will of Allah, yes." Her frown returned instantly. "But will you deny that you have a choice in all the matters that you make in this life? So yes, it is the will of Allah but you made a choice and that you have to deal with."

"What I have a choice to do is to ask for forgiveness and accept whatever comes from that."

Zaynab seemingly was done with Umar and his reasoning. She placed her balled fists in her lap, countered their discussion with a tight grin, and faced Celine. "In any case, Celine, welcome to the family inshallah you'll be taking Shahada, very soon."

"I intend on learning more about the religion and then making a decision from there."

His mother didn't say anything.

"That's all that can be done. The effort from there is in Allah's hands," his father said. "We will all be making dua that your heart is softened towards Islam. In shaa Allah you will do the same as you learn more about it. Pray that you will be guided to what is best for you."

Celine really liked how kind his father was and how he seemed to always choose his words wisely before speaking. Obviously Umar had inherited Zaynab's communication and peoples skills.

"Just make sure you're doing it for the right reasons." Zaynab brashly added.

Celine forced a smile. "That's why I want to take my time. To make sure it's in my heart and not only on my head."

"I respect that, dear." Mr. Talb said.

Celine never felt so awful about anything in her life. Zaynab made her feel ashamed of the person she'd been raised to be. As if she was an indecent person and less than the righteous Talb family. It was nothing she could do about being pregnant. In just a few short months from today they'd have to accept her and the baby as well.

Dinner ended not long after the baby interruption and she couldn't have been happier to get out of the Talb home. Two good things did come out of the horrid dinner party; now all of the cards were on the table, and witnessing Umar stand up for Celine made her feel a lot closer to him. Close enough to come forthright and reveal the impending court date just in case things didn't go as planned. This was the perfect time to do so, in fact. They'd just shared a bonding moment that signified Umar would stand up for her and now that his parents knew about the baby and their plans to wed, he'd have no choice but to deal with the outcome and go forth with their plans.

C28

"Thanks," Celine said.

They were sailing at a moderate speed down Baltimore Pike, just a few short blocks away from University City. The traffic was mild and weather relaxing, adding a soothing calm to their semi-turbulent evening at the Talb's.

"Thanks for what?"

"For the baby and I. For standing up for us."

"No need to say, thank you. I was just doing what I was supposed to do."

"I understand, but you didn't have to. I know how much you respect and love your mother."

"I do respect and love my mother. I also know when it comes to certain matters you have to put your foot down with women." He side eyed Celine. "My mother is a good woman and she will learn to adore you in time, in shaa Allah. You'll have to give her time and patience." He sighed. "Growing up, my mother always talked about having a good Muslim wife and marrying the ideal woman. It was embedded in us. Marriage was not something we wished upon a star on, it was what we were raised to partake in just as you're expected to walk your first steps; it was just the next phase of life. In her mind and heart she raised her sons to be good husbands. You can imagine the heartbreak she's feeling. I'm sure my mother takes our relationship very personal, as if she failed as a Muslim woman and parent."

Celine tried to understand Zaynab, but she honestly didn't. It wasn't as if he had done anything that was so shameful; Maly certainly didn't react and feel so disappointed. Zaynab was being self-righteous and overbearing. Umar still intended to marry Celine, only first came the carriage then the marriage.

"You also have to understand," Umar said as if he read her thoughts, "my parents have never known anyone in our family to *not* do things the traditional way. They come from a long line of traditional, Islamic family dealings. We don't have babies outside of marriage. That's just not acceptable."

Celine really wanted to say there's a first time for anything but she kept quiet and waited for Umar to finish up.

"She'll come around eventually. My mother needs to see how good of a person you are, and like I said when you take shahada and we're married I know she'll feel a lot better about you."

Maybe this wasn't the time for breaking news about the upcoming court date. Then again Celine needed the money as soon as possible. Twisting her puckered lips and gazing out of the passenger's window, Celine began to rethink her initial plans to come clean.

"I pray she will learn to love me and have a heart of forgiveness just as you do." Celine kept her eyes on the three-story houses and mix of Indian and Islamic shops and eateries they passed.

"I try to be as forgiving as possible, but it isn't something that comes naturally."

Celine nodded and agreed. "There isn't much I can say about that, we all struggle in that area. So far you have proven to be a pretty forgiving person through some of my intentional stunts. My guess would be you'd be even more forgiving if something occurred that wasn't intentional at all."

"In shaa Allah." His flat reply was questionable.

"Umar, I need to tell you something I haven't been able to get off of my chest."

"What's that?"

Celine tapped her foot and gnawed on her lip before taking in a breath that was supposed to prepare her for what she was about to say. "The night I found out about the baby I went out with Bella and Angelique to a club opening."

"That's not unusual for you." Umar's snide retort was obnoxious.

"No," she said, "it's not unusual behavior, but I was really drunk that night—"

"And? Is there something wrong with the baby you need to tell me?"

Fret was plastered all over his face.

"Oh no," she said. "The baby is perfectly fine, to my knowledge anyways."

"So what's the problem?"

"Remember when you were in Virginia and I called your phone over and over again? It was because I'd been arrested for public drunkenness."

"Arrested?"

"Yes, I was arrested for public drunkenness but that's not really the issue."

Growing impatient, Umar stepped on the brake and gave Celine a look that told her he had officially run out of patience. "If that's not the issue what is?"

"The issue is you know I'm not really considered a US citizen. Public drunkenness is considered a felony. I have a pending court date, which by the looks of it, I have a really good chance at getting off with probation. The downside is if things don't go as the lawyer and I hope, this is going to jeopardize my citizenship."

"You're telling me there's a possibility that you may have to leave the country?"

"I don't know, Umar, honestly. I have to go to court to figure this mess out. As I said I have a lawyer I've been talking to and—"

"And now you're sitting here telling me about this months later? When is your court date?" Angrily shifting from brake to acceleration, Umar shook his head and peeled off at the light.

"It's in just a few weeks, but if you could just listen I can explain to you—"

"Let you explain?" He laughed as if to say the request was ridiculous. "You have known about this for how many months and you're just now telling me you may have to leave the country? It's a never ending game with you, Celine. Why can't you be upfront and honest about the things you do?"

Appalled, Celine gasped. "I have been upfront and honest with you, Umar, and I think I've been quite patient and forgiving with you and some of your ways as well."

"It's been one big game with you. We have a baby on the way and you thought this was something you should withhold? No matter what, it's all one big mind game of manipulation. This is serious, Celine. How can you expect me to trust you to be honest with me now?"

"I am being honest with you. You can go to the lawyer's office with me. I need some help paying for the lawyer fees—"

He shook his head. "I get it now. You want to be honest because you need money?"

"It's not like that."

"Don't tell me what it's not like. You just made it clear. If you didn't need the money you would have continued to lie until the big secret surfaced."

Celine frowned at Umar. "Can you blame me for keeping something from you? You're so perfect in every way, Umar. You and your family think you all are so flawless."

He balled his hand into a fist and punched the horn. "Don't try to bring all my flaws or my family into this situation you tossed yourself into. How much money do you need me to leave for you to tell the truth?"

Celine dug her back against the seat and folded her arms over her chest. She shouldn't have said anything to Umar's judgmental-behind, at all. It would've been a lot simpler and less confrontational if Celine followed her instincts to speak with Khalid as she planned and together come up with their own scheme. Umar was just too critical. Celine had grown tired of hearing about all of her wrongs. She'd wait for him to drive through a couple more lights before answering any of his badgering.

"I asked how much money do you need, Celine, because I'm not going through this with you."

Celine twisted her neck in his direction. "What do you mean you're not going through this with me, Umar?"

"I just went toe to toe with my mother and father defending your honor and you haven't been upfront and honest with me during the past couple of months. I tried to give this relationship the benefit of doubt. I tried to give you the benefit of doubt and your intentions. I'm just confused."

"What have I done that's confused you?"

"Lying, scheming and manipulating from the first time I've met you in order to be with me."

"Umar, you are blowing this all the way out of proportion. I never tried to manipulate you. You're being extremely rude and inconsiderate to my feelings." Celine ignored the watering of her eyes. He was taking stabs at her intentions with him and made it seem as if she intentionally became pregnant. Deep down inside, she knew he'd always feel that way.

Umar drove to the apartment building and double parked. Pressing the button to prompt his flashers, he said, "How much?"

"A couple thousand."

"A couple thousand, Celine, just to pay off the lawyer and you don't even know what the outcome is going to be?"

"Yes," she mumbled.

"How about I do you one better? Since you have to pay off lawyer fees, I guess we'll postpone the wedding."

Painfully hurt, Celine frowned at Umar. "I don't see how paying the lawyer has anything to do with our wedding, Umar."

"Do you think I'm going to give you all the privileges you want-a beautiful wedding to show off to your friends, and pay for a lawyer?"

"I am not a child, Umar, I don't need to be punished."

"Well you're not acting like a woman right now, either, getting drunk and arrested."

"It was innocent. I had to go to the bathroom it's not like I was acting disorderly. This however, is very intentional, and controlling. My mother said you men tend to be that way."

He didn't respond to that.

Umar extended himself over the center console, undid the lock on the glove compartment, and removed his checkbook. Taking a pen out of the cup holder, he quickly scribbled on the check, ripped it from the book, and handed it to Celine.

"The five-thousand dollars was going to go towards a small reception and your ring, which would have been your dowry if you accepted it, of course. I had been planning a proper proposal and getting some things together to surprise you," he said, "but you can have it. We won't need it anymore."

They both looked at the check.

"Umar, what are you trying to say?"

"I'm saying I can't make a good woman out of somebody that's not ready to be one."

Celine bit her tongue and swallowed the hateful and foul things she wanted to say, that would only prove him right. "You are being extremely harsh right now."

"I'm going to send Khalid to get the rest of my stuff. I just want move back into my apartment and have peace during Ramadan."

"You can't have peace with me around?"

"Obviously not. Ramadan is starting soon and I've already sinned so much and repenting isn't working because I keep falling back into the same wrong space I was in when I started. I have no business staying with you, anyways. You're not going to understand."

Tears fell from her eyes. "Fine. If that's how you want it you enjoy your little Ramadan and life by yourself. Don't talk to me or the baby for an entire month. Go focus on Umar and how great of a person you pretend to be. Maybe in thirty days you'll actually be the man you think you are."

"Hurry up and clear the check before the money is transferred."

Celine wanted to smash the check in his face, but she needed it.

"Let me know the next time you have a doctor appointment, please? I'll be sure to be there."

"You're seriously considering calling off getting married? I believe you've been looking for every reason to do so and you found one, finally."

"Does it matter what I've been looking to do? What does matter is that I was trying to do what was right."

Celine shrieked as her body quivered with anger. "You have so many issues. Try working on yourself before you try to work on me. Please don't do me or the baby any favors. Follow your heart."

"If I followed my heart I would've married Tara by now."

"I hate you, Umar."

"What you need to work on," he said before he reached over Celine and unlocked the car door, "is figuring out how to keep out of prison."

C29

The only person Umar could think to call right now was Tara. After the first ring Tara accepted the call, but the line was full of dead air. Her breathing was barely audible. She was still waiting for an apology from the last time they'd spoken.

Clearing his throat and readjusting his broken posture, Umar made himself comfortable behind the wheel of the car for a not-so comfortable conversation. "I was hoping you could lend some words of support and encouragement."

She still didn't say anything.

"I know you're upset and disappointed with me but I just need someone to talk to, that's all, nothing more nothing less."

"Where are you?"

"I'm parked outside of my apartment."

"Come here and talk to me." Tara's gentle command was enticing, but he knew it wasn't meant to be more than a friendly gesture.

"It's ten o'clock and I don't want to disrespect your family."

"I'll let them know you're on your way. We can sit outside, on the steps. They know you, Umar, and for some reason trust you."

"Okay, I'm on my way."

Umar took the short drive about five minutes away from his apartment and parked two doors down from Tara's parents' house. He traveled down the street, past a few random neighbors, and embraced the calm of the fostering neighborhood. It was exactly how he'd remembered it. Towering, plush trees aligned the city streets, three-story homes made of stone and brick, and wide traffic lanes kept the area's diverse, historic look clean and classic. It was a neighborhood he'd grown up in close to masjids, halal eateries, shops and other local venues to enjoy. Umar remained close by, just on the other side of University City, but he was surrounded by more of the collegiate features of the area. Tara's family lived mixed with the new wave of University students that abandoned the tall homes once summer vacation began and the old residents that used to babysit them and where they'd spent many summer nights playing tag.

Tara was seated on her porch steps when he'd arrived. The light wasn't on, but the street lights gave just enough light to illuminate her delicate features. Gorgeously wrapped in a black shayla draped over her matching abaya which flowed to her hip and onto the cemented porch, Umar tried not to stare too hard but he couldn't help it. It was something about Tara that tugged at his heart. The same feeling he couldn't shake as a kid watching her blossom into a young, intelligent, and independent woman she'd become. Tonight she was even more beautiful than before. No makeup, eyeliner, or mascara; she looked as if she pulled herself out of bed just to sit and talk to him. He knew she did. Tara was a modest woman, yet, still a bit of a beauty queen. To see her in her natural state, just for him, had his emotions ready to cuddle her and tell her all the things a woman of her statue needed to hear.

"As salaamu alaikum."

"Wa alaikum salaam." Her reply was flat, but it was a false representation of her true feelings. Allowing him to visit her at such late hours was evidence that she didn't feel as hard as she pretended.

"Tara, I really just want to apologize-"

"I don't want your apology."

"But I want to—"

"You needed me to lend an ear because you're heartbroken and going through some rough troubles not because you wanted to apologize. So please, go on with your story."

"Do you really have to be so cold?"

She sucked her teeth with a long roll of the eyes. "What else would you like me to be?"

"I don't know, at least a little more understanding? I'm trying to open up to you." Umar's arms went from by his side to guarding his chest. Leering at her, a little annoyed, he nibbled at the inside of his cheek and went over the decision he'd made of calling Tara knowing they had unresolved issues. He was starting to regret confiding in Tara. She was bitter.

"What you're trying to do is open up to me over a relationship matter that doesn't concern me, at all. The issue is another woman-not a problem between you and I. If you want a friend to listen, you have it, but don't expect me to disregard my feelings."

"If you're not going to do that then why did you call me over here?"

"Because you needed me, Umar. Take what you can get and be happy."

Take what you can get and be happy? This was not the Tara he knew. She never talked to him this way. Heck, he'd never seen her upset with him in all the years he'd known her, she was always Miss forgiving. Umar admired her hard look and closed-off body language though, it was a turn on. Something about seeing how much she cared made him want her more. The challenge she now presented was alluring. Smiling at the way he suddenly felt towards Tara, Umar hastily looked away at the cars zooming by.

"What are smiling about, Umar? I'm serious, take what you can get and be happy. Now what's the problem?"

He chuckled then smiled at Tara.

She shook her head. "I'm pretty sure if you really needed someone to talk to you would have called Celine, but obviously she is the problem if you called me. So go ahead and talk."

It wasn't much for him to say in response to that.

Umar hiked one foot on the step where Tara's feet rested and slid his hands deep into his pockets.

"Shhhh," he said. "Don't talk so much, it's un-lady like." Right away Tara's frown loosened to a smirk and then a slow, exasperated breath. "Everyone around me seems to be getting into some type of trouble and I'm just trying to keep my head held high."

"I don't know what you want me to say. You can't allow other people's problems to be your burden. In all fairness to the people you're referring to, Umar, you haven't been a saint yourself."

"Yeah but, there's an issue with Celine she's gotten into that may affect the baby."

Tara sat quiet.

"I know you may not care too much about the baby or anything having to do with kids, but this is a big deal for me."

"What would make you think that I don't care about the baby?"

Umar shrugged. "I mean-I guess I just assumed."

"I'm not a cold hearted person, Umar. You have a baby on the way alhumdullah. I am disappointed in you for how it happened, but that has nothing to do with the baby. Yes, I was hurt when I found out, but I'm not mad over a child, Umar, I'm mad you lied." She paused. "I'd pray if I would ever have a child you would be happy for me as well."

"I didn't think you wanted children?" he said quizzically.

Tara's neck pulled back, her brows crumpled with confusion. "What would give you that impression?"

He never thought to double check what Celine told him or even if there was more to the story. He also knew not to mention what Celine had said. It would open a new can of worms between him and Tara. It was not an option. They were making progress, and he was actually enjoying the open conversation they were currently having; more than that, the potential of where the conversation could go.

It would be better to be direct instead of beating around the bush. "Do you want children, Tara?"

"To be honest with you, Umar, I would love to have children, but I don't think I can."

"Why do you think that?"

Tara wrapped the shayla around her tighter, hugged her body, and sighed. "The reason I divorced was because of my pregnancy. After I had a tubular pregnancy and several failed attempts to carry after that, my husband said he wasn't going to be able to have the dream child he wanted to have with me."

"Oh," Umar said apologetically.

"It became increasingly depressing, for both of us. It may have been my test, but I couldn't stand seeing how disappointed he was every time I lost a baby. He couldn't take me getting so down and out every time I miscarried as well. It was a huge toll."

"That was the dream you spoke of?"

"Yes, I just couldn't give him his dream baby. We tried and we tried for the first two years of our marriage, but we lost three babies after the first."

He was studying to be an Imam. It was extremely important to him to have a child and for us to be a role model for the community. He couldn't be such a strong community leader without any heir to his name."

"That's not true, Tara, you should know better than that. Your marriage could've been a great inspiration for couples struggling in the same department."

"It was, masha Allah, but that didn't stop his desire for wanting children. When he decided to take another wife it was just too much for me to handle. The thought of her having a baby by him," Tara dropped her gaze and curtly shook her head, "I couldn't handle it."

Umar felt bad for being so curious about her divorce and not being sensitive to Tara's desire to keep it private. It was painful and something she was ashamed of. He then thought about his own situation and how hard it must've been for Tara when she found out he was having a baby knowing she may not have the ability to give him one even if they were to marry.

"Tara," he said, "I didn't know, sorry."

She rolled her eyes. "It wasn't something for you to know or anyone else," she said. "I was a little jealous when I found out about Celine. I even questioned if I would be able to be in a relationship with you, despite you having a baby with someone else."

"I'm sure it would be too hard for you to handle." Although he was hoping to hear otherwise.

"I don't know." Tara grinned. "It's something I'll pray on—my jealousy. I'm trying to accept I may not be able to have children little by little and grow every day. It's hard to understand what is for me is for me and is from Allah. That may sound easy, but it's not. As women we're taught we're supposed to have babies, and that it's a major part of our role in society and in our families; every woman should aspire to be a mother and wife. Some decide not to by choice, masha Allah, but to know that I'll never be able to fill the role possibly, and not by choice," she sighed, "that is very hard for me to swallow."

Umar wished he could reach out, hold her in his arms and tell her everything would be alright. She touched him in a new way and he just knew he had to have her as his wife—somehow. For now he would keep his distance and remain respectful, but mentally Umar was planning his next move.

They both remained still.

"Is there anything else you had to tell me about Celine?"

"Nothing. I don't want to talk about her right now."

"You're here," she said, "what do you want to talk about?

Umar smiled and sat on the steps. "Africa."

"Africa?" she said, gathering the lines in her forehead as she broke into an amused chuckle that automatically lightened up the mood between them.

"Yes," Umar said with a big grin, "Africa. Remember the conversation we had about me possibly taking the job at SFN?"

"Na'am."

"I'm considering it since Celine said she may have to move back to Canada. Africa may really be on the plate."

Bewildered, Tara's eyes opened widely. "What would make her move to Canada?"

"I really don't think this is the time to tell you her business."

"I'll accept that," she said, and he was glad. "So tell me more about Africa?"

Umar's brows furrowed. "Do you think you would be interested in moving to Africa?"

"I thought we already discussed you have a baby on the way."

"And," he said, "I thought you just made it clear you're trying to get over your jealousy and the possibility to marry someone who already has children?"

Tara huffed then smiled avoiding eye contact with Umar.

"We can't move to Africa, Umar," she said, her cheeks glowing in the light from the street poles.

"Why not? You married someone and traveled across the country, what is another continent?"

"Are you serious, Umar?"

He laughed at her disgust. "Yes," he said, still laughing, "I am."

"Don't compare this situation to my past marriage, it's way different. Besides, there's so much to do here. I just can't see myself picking up and leaving."

"What do you have that would hold you back? You have a new job you just started—"

"And my family?"

"They're not going anywhere, in shaa Allah."

"But I can't move across the world and leave my family behind, Umar."

"You'll have a new family, in shaa Allah."

"Umar, you can't just show up at my door one night with your problems from your other relationship and think you're going to start a new one with me."

"That's not what this is."

Tara stood shaking her head and reworked her shayla. "If not, then what are you doing right now?"

"Right now," Umar said and stood, "I'm stepping up to the plate and doing what I wanted to do for the past couple of months. All I've been doing is trying to please everyone else. I need to focus on pleasing myself and Allah. I tried to please Celine and received nothing but drama. I tried to please Khalid and found myself living on Celine's couch which totally goes against what I should be doing as a Muslim and as a provider. Now what I really want to do is please myself and focus on pleasing the number one person that's been on my mind, which will also allow me to please my Lord."

"You're going to have to give me a lot of time to think about something like this."

"No," Umar sternly countered. "I'm not giving you too much time, Ramadan is almost here. I'm going to give you a month of space to think, pray and figure out if you think you could be happy with me."

"Things are not that simple, Umar."

"It can be," he said. "I'll see you in thirty days."

C30

"Angelique," Celine sobbed into the phone, "I really think this time it's over. He was so upset with me. I even told him to stay out of our lives for not being compassionate."

She gasped. "How can he be so upset, it was just an accident?"

Celine nodded and used the back of her hand to sweep away a tear. "That's exactly how I feel. I think he was still edgy after defending me against his parents. Then hearing that I've done something to jeopardize my citizenship, and possibly our child's—" Celine wiped another fallen tear, "he just seemed to explode."

Angelique sighed into the phone. "Just give him time, Celine."

That sounded like a good idea, but for the first time since they'd begun their relationship Celine was totally pessimistic about having a future with Umar. She didn't see it happening, ever. Not only did she not have hopes of patching things up between them, but she didn't think time would be in her favor.

"He gave the money to pay for my trial." Celine sniffled.

"That's a start."

"It's a start but it wasn't given happily. For all I know it could be his way of cutting ties with me. He said it would've been my dowry."

Angelique hummed into the phone. "Is he saying that giving you the money solidified the marriage and that you'd no longer receive the dowry, or the wedding is off?"

As embarrassed as she felt, Celine had to be honest.

"I'm pretty sure he meant the wedding is off."

She gasped again, this time sharper with repulsion. "Oh no, you must be devastated."

"I don't know how to feel right now. There are so many different things in my head. I just want to feel happy, ya know?"

"I certainly do. If it makes you feel better I want to take you shopping for the baby soon."

"I would love that."

Shopping would have made Celine feel better three weeks ago. Now with the mounting pressure of the baby and court, going shopping wasn't close to being on the forefront of her mind.

"Hold on, Angelique, Bella is calling."

"It's late. How about you call me tomorrow? We'll talk about this some more. I still want to take you shopping."

"I think I would like that. Thanks so much. I love you, Angelique."

"I love you too."

They said goodbyes and Celine switched to Bella.

"Celine-pooh, what's wrong? You never call me this late at night."

Celine put the phone on speaker and looked at the time. It was nearly 12 a.m. She'd been on the phone crying almost an hour and hadn't noticed.

"I know. I'm sorry, but thanks for returning my phone call. I'm just so upset."

"Does this have something to do with Umar?"

"Yes, it does but really it's my fault. I finally told him about the upcoming case and when I was arrested."

Bella shockingly sucked in a heap of air. "What did he say?"

"He said a whole lot. Umar called off the engagement between us."

She gasped again and in a whiny but empathetic tone said, "I'm sure he'll come back around."

"I'm going to pay the lawyer and ask Umar to go with me. Maybe once the lawyer explains things to him he'll see it really wasn't my fault."

"If I was you I would be happy he gave the money for the lawyer and leave it at that."

Confused, Celine's lips contorted with displeasure at Bella's advice. "Why would you suggest that?"

"Because," Bella chided, "as much as I love you, Celine and as much as I hate to say it—Umar has been nothing but a headache ever since you've been pregnant. All the stress and pressure you feel has come from trying to be good to him. If I was you, which I'm partially glad I'm not, I would pack my emotional bags and leave it alone. Plenty of women these days raise their child without a man in the home. You're beautiful, intelligent, and educated. Celine you have a great job and are on your way to doing great things. If you ask me, you don't need him or the headache he brings."

Celine didn't need him. Yes, she could do it solo, but why? She didn't want to do it all alone. A nice job and all the great qualities mentioned didn't compare to marital security. The security of having a great spouse and father was something she longed for since she was a little girl. It was one of the many things her childhood lacked, yet the number one factor which still affected her to this day.

"I don't fully agree with what you're saying, but I understand your point of view."

"Just think about it. You told me it's been drama tale after drama tale. Don't forget he's in love with that Tara girl."

Celine regretted opening her big mouth to her so called friend. Bella was doing a poor job of encouraging her at the moment. Going on about Tara was of no benefit. She didn't want to hear about Tara or any other woman, and she wasn't asking for advice to walk away, Celine simply wanted a friend.

"You know Bella, I really feel like sometimes you can be very insensitive."

"I'm not insensitive."

"You are," Celine coldly replied. "I'm trying to pour my heart out to you, about my man and my situation, and you're busy tossing another woman in my face."

"I'm just trying to be a good friend."

"A good friend would understand just how much I want to have a family and that I want my child to have what I didn't have growing up."

"I get it, Celine, but everything we do as adults can't be based upon what we missed as a child. I'm just trying to support you."

Celine was growing utterly annoyed and was over the conversation. "Support me by telling me how to smooth things over with him and how to make my family work. Not by finding a reason to keep us separated."

"I understand everything you're saying but I just want you to know you always have options, and being hurt in a relationship that is not good for you is not the best option to take."

Celine released a low groan.

"We both came from single-parent households and turned out just fine," Bella added, "so why are you so scared to do it just like your mother did?"

"Because," Celine said, "my mother spent the rest of her life trying to find a man to love her and only ended up with enough children to set up a basketball starting lineup. Yes, I can do it by myself. And yes I could be like my mother, but the question is do you really think that's what I want? To spend the rest of my life searching for someone to love me all because I had a child by another man before we decided to get married?"

"I'm sorry, you're right."

"Why spend the rest of my life searching for someone to love me when I could busy myself mending the relationship with someone that already has a connection with me?"

The sound of the other line sounded again, this time it was Umar.

"Hey," Celine said, "that's Umar calling. I'm going to talk to you later."

"Hey Celine, we need to talk." He was kind of surprised Celine actually answered the phone after their spat.

"Yes, Umar?" she said. "First, let me say I'm sorry. I was totally wrong for keeping information from you but I just want to let you know I'm going to talk to the lawyer tomorrow. You should join me."

"I think it's good you're talking to the lawyer tomorrow, Celine, but I'm not going to go with you."

"Okay, so–"

"I want to talk to you about the possibility of moving back to Canada, it may not be such a bad idea."

"I can't believe you would say something like that." Celine started going into tears.

Despite his hard exterior and the way he'd handle Celine oftentimes, Umar really did hate to hear her cry. He swallowed the lump in his throat. "I have my reasons for it."

"I'm sure you have reasons," she cut him off, "but there's no reason for me to move so far when I have a baby on the way, no matter what you've conjured."

"I understand that," Umar said, "but if you would just listen and give me two minutes to explain."

"Go on," she said still whaling into the phone.

"I've been offered a great position with SFN, the sports network."

Stifling her cries, Celine sniffled and said, "That's great, Umar."

"It is," he said and sighed, "but the position is not in America, the position will be in Africa." Umar nervously cleared his throat. "Going back home will give you family support. It may be good for you and the baby. I can fly back and forth until the baby is old enough to visit."

"You think that'll be best, for you to leave the continent? We have a child, Umar, I need your help."

He knew she was right, but he also knew what was best. "This will be more money for you and for the baby, Celine. Soon I'll be able to provide for the baby in a way that will offer him, in shaa Allah, better than we both had and make your life a whole lot easier."

"When were you offered the position, Umar?"

Crumpling under the scrutiny that was sure to come, Umar said, "Shortly after I found out you were pregnant."

"You're upset with me for keeping secrets but you have been keeping this a secret the entire time?" Celine hotly exclaimed through the speaker.

"I wasn't positive about taking it."

"What changed?"

"My feelings," Umar bantered. He could feel heat in his face. The mix of shame and guilt swirled with the need to become the winner in this, who-was-wrong-first argument had his body tingling and tremor.

"Your feelings towards me or feelings towards the job?"

"You're making this harder than it should be," he said, glad he didn't have to look her in the eyes. "If you would just listen I can explain how this would be a benefit to both of us–"

"There would be a benefit in it if you allowed me to move to Africa with you, but you've already made it clear that you won't."

More tears flowed through the phone. Umar, however, was determined to keep calm and show little interest in her irrational emotions. In the process of getting to know Celine, he'd learned he had to be stern in every way with her–or any woman for that matter.

"You can't come with me. It's going to be too much of a hassle," he said, at least not right now. I'll be very busy starting a new career and I don't want you over there with a baby and the lack of support you'll need."

"But," she stammered, "if you're going to make much more money why can't we hire help? I'm sure it would be extremely affordable for us to afford a babysitter or someone that can assist me with the baby in Africa."

She had a good point. "In shaa Allah, that doesn't sound like a bad idea," he said, "but first I'll need to get everything established for us, Celine. Being that we'll have the baby soon, I think it is best for you to go home and allow your mom and family to help.

"You're breaking my heart," she said with hitching breaths.

Umar pulled the phone from his ear and wiped his clammy palms on his shirt. He hated breaking her heart. He knew it was the truth.

"I'll make sure I'm here for the next couple of months before the baby comes when I accept the job."

"Then after?"

"I'll do my best to make everything extremely comfortable. I promise I will not let you down and you'll be out to visit as soon as possible."

"This is unbelievable."

"If I was in the military or some type of famous performer you wouldn't mind me being gone for long periods of time. Just be patient."

"No," she menacingly spat. "I don't want to be patient. I'm tired. You're right, I am going to go back home. Once I go back home you'll never see the baby again."

"You're just upset right now, Celine–"

She then ended the call before he could respond.

C31

Celine hadn't been the same ever since Umar gave her the information about his new job. They hadn't talked much since then, either. He managed to call once a day to make sure she and the baby were well; however, that wasn't enough by Celine's standards. Only two days passed and already she missed him terribly. Celine felt awful for lying, keeping secrets, and taking her friends' advice. She felt even worse thinking about how she'd have to raise the baby alone, in Canada, while Umar lived handsomely on the other side of the world meeting his dreams. It was depressing. Life changing. Her life morphed into something that would make a scandalously juicy romance plot for a book or Lifetime movie, but not a lifestyle she'd want for her reality.

On the upside, the one thing adding a bit of light to Celine's dim, pathetic world was that right now she sat twirling her gentle curls around her fingers, admiring the latest issue of Health and Fitness magazine in Mr. Bradshaw's office. She was anxious. Cutting the sleeze-bucket a check for five-thousand dollars paid in full, wasn't exactly how Celine would've spent the amount of money under normal circumstances—by any means, yet the coils of relief that sprang in her stomach were unexpectedly similar to that of spontaneously purchasing a pair of Prada pumps from another person's bank account. Prada. It had been quite some time since Celine opted to splurge on a new pair of shoes, and with the baby due in a few short months it would probably be a very long time before she'd have the additional income to treat herself to such jewels. She flipped the page and skimmed over a recipe for vegetarian tacos with an emerging grin brimming her face. Shoes could wait. Signing the paperwork and solidifying the end of project-deport-Celine was such a phenomenal burst of butterflies it could've sent her into premature labor.

Not too long after taking a snapshot of the taco recipe the receptionist called Celine to visit Mr. Bradshaw. Quickly, she noted that he'd worn the same suit he'd chosen for their last encounter. Unsure how'd she'd felt about his lack of wardrobe or his carefree attitude for being seen in the same outfit in such a close amount of time, Celine pushed the thought to the side for later investigation and took a seat. Paying attention to little details such as wardrobe rotation could mean he'd overlook details for her. If it weren't for the clock ticking on her hearing, without a doubt she would've questioned Mr. Bradshaw about his attire.

"I just want you to know you should be one hundred percent confident about getting off with merely probation. I've already spoken to the judge and she gave me the heads up. You're in the clear, Celine." Confidence spilled from his mouth excitedly and had Celine sliding to the edge of her chair to make sure she'd heard correctly. This was perfect. She removed the check from her purse ready to hand it over. With her hands cupped over her knees, Celine took a sigh of relief.

"Wow," she said, "I'm surprised you were able to do so much for so little."

"She owed me a favor," Mr. Bradshaw smugly assured her. "Not to mention I really want to see you and the baby do well here. I can't imagine you having to live in another country away from your boyfriend."

Celine fanned her lashes and stared blankly at Mr. Bradshaw at the mention of the word boyfriend. It was almost as if he'd had some type of fortunetelling ability. She *would* be living in another country away from Umar, if God allowed it. Handing over the five-thousand dollars suddenly seemed to be a waste of hard earned cash. What was her endgame now? With or without Mr. Bradshaw's help, Celine would eventually separate from the man she'd wanted to stay in the country for. She pinched the check between her fingers tighter. With the new reality Umar shoved her way, perhaps saving the money and moving would've been best. Before she'd second guess herself, again, Celine gave the check to Mr. Bradshaw and slid her back into the chair.

"Now that everything is all squared away, I'll see you in two more weeks, Celine."

"Mr. Bradshaw, if we already know I'm getting off with probation why do I have to show up to the court date?"

"I know and you know is like smelling the ammonia when we enter a kitchen," he said, "but we still have to make sure everything is clean."

Celine didn't quite understand his analogy, but said, "I can see how that makes sense."

"Just leave everything to me, Celine. I told you I'll have this all handled. The only thing I want you to worry about is what type of crib you're going to purchase for that beautiful baby of yours."

Celine smiled. "I don't think I can thank you enough for helping me."

"No thanks needed. It's my job."

"This won't completely be washed from your record, but I'm sure you can agree that probation is a lot better than jail time, and also a lot better than deportation."

She nodded. "I agree."

"Good," he said and stretched his hand over the enclave for a handshake. Right away, Umar and his explanation of why women shouldn't shake hands with men sprang into her thoughts. "I will see you there in a couple weeks and square all of this away."

A shock of electricity zipped throughout her limbs arousing an overwhelming sense of gratitude and satisfaction. Things weren't looking too good for her social life. Just knowing she'd accomplished one thing that consequently affected her child's life, felt great. Celine couldn't wait to tell Umar the great news. He hadn't accepted the job, yet. Maybe this was God's way of giving them a fresh start. Ramadan was starting tomorrow and she knew Umar would surely be focused on getting events together for the community. This was a great time to share their blessings. This was also a great time for her to focus and better herself. Get closer to God. Allah. Yes, she would honestly focus on giving Islam a chance and showing Umar she was a woman of her word. Just the week prior, he'd given her a book for new shahadas. At the time she'd stacked it in her closet along with other educational books she'd collected over the years, but now things would be different. The book would be dusted off and visually digested. She intended to study and learn as much as she could in the next thirty days. Everything was now cleared up. It was time to step her game up, again, and do everything she needed to do to secure her future husband.

C32

Everything had gone through as promised and Celine assured Mr. Bradshaw she'd refer anyone to him that was in need of his services. Ramadan had come and finally came to close. Umar managed to keep the distance he'd said he would during the holy month. Aside from occasional text messages and one trip to the doctor, she hadn't seen much of him. His unyielding devotion to the month only made her crave him even more. It was admirable and sexy, if you asked her. Most of all, it was undoubtedly a quality she'd want in her man. There was also the book she vowed to study and read with an open mind that softened her heart towards Umar. There was way more to the religion than she'd initially thought. No, Islam was a way of life that required Celine to step outside of herself and spend more time to think long and hard about what was societal norms and what was that from a higher power. The startling realization was scary and not one she would've ever ventured into rationalizing had it not been for her unexpected pregnancy by a man which she'd known prior to their mishap was sculpted by greatness. It was what attracted her to Umar and what kept her yearning for him. His balance.

His piety. His desire to be great and better than he was the day before, while taking little to no accountability for all of the precious things he'd been blessed with.

Celine finished the last paragraph in the book for new Shahadas and snapped it shut, ecstatic to call Umar and discuss all of the wonderful things she'd learned and her new level of appreciation and understanding for what he held so dear. The last night of Ramadan was the night prior. From her understanding, the majority of the Muslim world would be at a unified prayer, then off to celebrate the end of the month. It was one of the few holidays, if one should call it that, that she'd read about for the Islamic religion. The way Celine saw it, accomplishing thirty days of going without food or water from sun up to sun down was more than something to celebrate.

Reaching for her phone, Celine glanced at the time. By 12PM Umar should've been well into the festivities. Calling him shouldn't have been an issue.

Urgently, her cell phone rang. It was her mother. Twisting her lips nervously and gawking at the device, Celine allowed the ringer to chime as long as possible before the call ended. Maly would not be happy with Celine's new discovery. Life as Maly had presented it was semi-chaotic and the opposite of what she'd taught Celine in regards to spirituality and men. She couldn't imagine what disdained feelings her mother would have towards Celine, Islam, and her premature thoughts of Umar inevitably being controlling due to his upbringing. Come to think of it, Celine did know exactly what Maly would say; and that was exactly why her nerves were popping like fireworks.

"Celine," her mother started right away, "you never call. I've been worried about you and the baby. Has the father been keeping you away from us?"

"Umar, mother, has not kept and will not keep me away from my family. Family is a major part of his religion and very important to him."

"Hmph, I don't know if I agree with that. From what I've been told they will keep a woman away from her family, especially if the family does not believe in their God."

"It's the same God, mother."

"Says who? Celine, sweetie, I'm sorry. I just have been so concerned. You've neglected all my calls."

Maly was right and was worried within reason. Celine had ignored many of her calls in the past few weeks as she studied. She wanted to have a clear mind as she learned about Islam without any outside influences. Maly had a way of making Celine feel guilty and second guess any of her decisions.

"You're right, mother, and I apologize for acting that way."

"This is a pleasant surprise," she was being snide. "It's a rarity to hear you own up to avoiding my calls."

"I'm turning over a new leaf."

"That's wonderful, Celine, because I have turned over one as well."

Celine laughed to herself cynically. "Oh?"

"Yes," he mother said. "I've realized just how horrible I've been with introducing different men into my children's lives. Well, I've always known it wasn't best, but it was a means to an end. Now, however, that has changed. Remember the man I told you purchased the game system for your brother?"

"The married one?"

"Stop that, Celine," she snickered. "I can hear the negative energy through the phone."

"I'm sorry," she said, this time pleasant and enthusiastic, "the married one?"

"No," she snipped, "because he is no longer married. I had a long hard talk with him. We both decided it would be best for him to leave his wife and for him to make an honest woman out of me."

"You've got to be kidding."

"I am not. I deserve happiness, Celine, and he knows it. I've been beyond devoted to caring and listening to his daunting tales of his miserable marriage for the past few months. The least he could do is get rid of her and fall into the arms of the better woman."

"That would be you, I'm assuming?"

Maly sucked her teeth. "There are some things you haven't grown to mature and understand yet, Celine."

Disturbed, Celine brushed off her mother's laughable notion. "Mother, I've been learning a lot of Islam and—"

"Not you too," she said.

"What do you mean?"

"These men have been convincing women to jump the Jesus ship and sail to hell. I've been seeing it all over Toronto."

"That's a crude accusation don't you think?"

"No," she said, "I don't."

"Mother,"

"You haven't graced the aisle of a mosque yet and you're ready to devote yourself to a new religion? At least make him put a ring on it."

"We've discussed marriage, mother, you already know this."

"Discussing marriage and being married are not the same. Hmph, you don't see me jumping ship to be with a man, do you? Once we're officially married then I will trust and commit myself to any necessary changes. Until then, I am the prize and I must be constantly competed for. Don't make yourself so easy,

Celine. You're already carrying the man's baby. Now you want to change your entire life to suit him? I've raised you to be better than that."

Celine was dismayed and utterly offended by Maly's way of thinking. This from a woman whom was currently engaged to a man that Celine could bet her last dollar was not out of his marriage, yet—if he'd opt out of it at all.

"Mother, I have to go."

"I think that would be a good idea, Celine. You really need to give more thought to all of the life changes you're putting yourself through. I only want what's best."

"I understand."

"I love you ."

"Love you as well, mom."

C33

It was close to two months later Celine concluded she was ready to convert to Islam. It was an amazing feeling, accepting God in her life in a manner that gave her the much needed discipline that would sculpt her lifestyle as well as her growing baby. There was so much to learn and understand. Beforehand, many of the routines and obligations seemed burdensome. Unattainable you could even say. After learning, thinking, rethinking, and secluding herself from Bella, Angelique, Maly, and even Umar, adjusting to the simpler way of life that Islam presented appeared to be more than possible. Her fancy way of dress had eased into a modest version of itself effortlessly, and even her ability to control her impulsive behavior whenever Umar didn't do exactly what she'd asked had come to a gentle simmer. Ironically, Celine's handling things in such a cool manner aroused more questions out of Umar than her erratic actions in the past. This new way of living made her feel radiant and full of life. Finally, she was ready to reveal to Umar just what was causing her to feel so fantastic.

Things hadn't changed much since she and Umar had their quarrel in the car; in some ways their relationship had changed for the better. Umar kept his distance from Celine which ultimately lead to less fights, friendlier visits, and gave Celine a greater appreciation for the failed relationship they'd tried to have earlier in her pregnancy. She still desired Umar in every way possible, and she hadn't given up on their engagement. Celine understood now more than ever that her role as a woman was to bring peace to his life. Umar was a great provider and made sure Celine wanted for nothing and always answered when she'd call. He too had made great changes. These changes made her even more hopeful for their future, together.

Making herself comfortable in her desk's chair, a task that was becoming harder by the day, Celine added another page to the article she'd been working on. Today was the start of the new year for Muslims, had she'd taken shahada and still worked at AME, today would've been a day off and reason to eat and receive gifts. She was grateful for her new job but secretly missed AME, especially with her on the verge of converting.

Regardless, Celine had very little to complain about. Her career had been sprouting, but Celine's Cuisine had taken a major turn in a way she'd never imagined. Her new column for Fashionably Fit Femmes brought a new fan base to her website. The column didn't focus on issues like Drama Mama. FFF focused on tricks of the trade for staying your best during and after having a baby. Celine of course was the featured model and blogger. Pregnant life had been good to Celine and she enjoyed sharing her secrets of fitness and beauty. Everything was blossoming lovely and Celine's new found way of thinking helped her to be humble and thankful for every bit of it.

A distracting barrage of alerts suddenly sent Celine's phone into an electronic frenzy. Whipping her neck to view the phone, Celine held it high and squinted at the screen. What in the world was so buzz worthy? Not only were the social network notifications dinging out of control, but her texts as well. Without question one reflected the other. Celine scrolled through the list and singled an alert on her Instagram. Someone tagged her on a video Umar posted ten minutes earlier.

She went to it.

Watched.

Like a serpent strangling her heart, a tense, suffocating pull caused Celine's heart to stop as she struggled to control her breath and anger. The video, that she was so kindly tagged in, was that of Umar asking Tara's father for her to be his wife, her unattractive father agreeing, and Tara giddily ogling Umar and accepting in front of a band of Muslims at the Eid festival.

Celine was livid.

Umar kept his secret intention to marry Tara out of every conversation they'd had over the past few months. Tara was a sneaky, horrible, woman. This was embarrassing. Her fans, his, and the rest of the world were witnessing Tara get swept off of her feet by Celine's child's father—while Celine was still with child. How disgusting! The two of them lovey dovey and the patrons clapping and congratulating their upcoming ceremony. Celine had seen enough.

She was not going to cry.

She refused to shed a tear.

A tear dropped then quickly she was over it.

Umar had deceived her beyond measure. This was not going to be taken lightly. All of the things she'd learned about anger and being a good person was out the window. These were horrible people. If this was how Muslims behaved, Celine wanted nothing to do with them or the religion.

Rifling through her photo album, Celine uploaded every picture and video she'd taken of her belly, Umar while he slept on her sofa, and other pictures that connected the two of them. No, they hadn't slept together since the baby, and yes, when he stayed at her apartment he never shared the bed with her, but so what? The pictures clearly indicated otherwise. She wouldn't be the only one embarrassed. The more pictures uploaded the more evil her thoughts brewed. These were just the start. There was absolutely no way she'd allow her child to enter the home of that man—stealing winch. Never. The two of them had another thing coming if they'd thought she'd sit back and watch Umar and Tara dance off into the moonlight of happily ever after. Celine promised to give him hell, and she was just warming up.

C34

Still wearing a fuchsia and white long-sleeved maxi dress with a train that dragged about a foot or two behind her, the same she'd worn to the Eid prayer and festival, Tara walked over to Umar holding a cup of hot green tea. He too was still cloaked in his dapper attire. The egg-shell colored thobe adorned with gold embroidered stitching along the collar and cuffs looked staggering on Umar. He'd also put on a few pounds in the best way possible. Indeed, when they stepped off of the plane and into the motherland, Umar wanted to look his best. The new diet and exercise regimen had paid off plentifully, now however, was time to celebrate and eat pie.

"I just don't know what to say, Tara," Umar stammered, "I apologize."

Tara sat across the kitchen table and placed the tea on the place mat. There were still a few guests in her parents' living room, and Umar's parents were there as well coercing about their pending marriage.

"I know it wasn't your fault."

"Alhumdullah, you're so wonderful."

"Umar," she cut him off with a perplexed look and a wave of her hand, "how long will this last?"

"I don't have an honest answer for that, Tara, Allahu alim."

"I understand that," she said, "but I have a reputation, too. Today she went on a rampage to embarrass both of us. This is just the beginning, you know? Women can be very spiteful. Maybe this isn't the right time for you and I."

"Are you saying that you're allowing her to get to you this early on?"

Tara, resentfully propped her elbow on the table, dug her chin into her palm, and huffed. "I'm not giving up on us, Umar, of course not. I just want to know how do you plan on handling this? I don't want to spend the rest of our lives battling Celine."

"You're exaggerating."

"Please don't undermine my feelings, Umar. I need to feel confident that you will have a talk with her."

"What will that do?"

"I'd hope she'd have enough decency to stop. You and she both have careers people follow. We also have a community to represent. Doesn't she understand you've already been warned by your boss?"

"Just give her time," he said.

"You're being passive."

"No, I'm being understanding and so should you. Let us both have more compassion. I don't have high expectations for her. You, on the other hand, I expect to represent yourself to a higher standard."

"That's unfair." Pouting, Tara moved her hands to hug her waist and slumped in the chair.

"That's what I expect of my future wife. Let me know now if you can't handle what life may bring."

"I told you I'm fine, just a little concerned. If the shoe were on the other foot I'm sure you'd feel the same."

Umar usually maneuvered his ailing temper with Tara, lately though, her nagging about Celine's position in his life fostered a new level of self control. He tried his best to exercise patience for Tara and Celine. Everything was very new for the both of them, and with Celine he had to try his best to deal with her hormonal mood swings. Tara was worked up over nothing. Shortly after the baby was born, which would only be a few months, Celine would learn to move on with her life and they'd co-parent in a healthy manner.

He slid his chair around the table and next to Tara's. He loved seeing her upset over their future. It told him she cared.

"Beautiful," he said lovingly, "you should be concerned. If it were the other way around, you're right, I probably would not sit at this table with your belly filled with another man's baby." They both chuckled. "That's not the case. All I can do is ask for forgiveness." Umar leered deeply into her eyes and admired her soft lips that shined with a faded hint of clear gloss. He licked his own and scooted the chair a little closer. "Let's get married tonight," he said.

Tara giggled. "Yeah right, Umar. Our parents would be so disappointed. They're looking forward to the walima more than we are."

"Who cares?" he said, then whispered, "if we were married I'd help you feel more secure about your place in my life."

She looked at him and frowned. "That wouldn't do the trick."

"Tricks are for magicians, Tara. I'm talking about treating you like a queen and crowning your highness."

They both laughed.

"Seriously," he said after harnessing his laughter, "The best treasure in the world is a righteous wife. In shaa Allah, that will be you very soon."

"In shaa Allah," she said.

"I'm going to talk to her. I think you should too."

"Me?"

"Yes," he said. "I'll arrange a meeting. It may be what's needed for you two. A formal introduction will help Celine feel included, in shaa Allah."

Tara sighed. "I'll do it, for you."

"Masha Allah, how about Friday?"

"I'll need more time than that. She just sought to embarrass us. Give me two more weeks, please?"

"Two more weeks it is. That'll be just a few weeks before the wedding. It would be nice for her to come."

She sighed. "I'm not sure how I feel about that, Umar."

"I understand."

"I'll have a talk with her, soon, I promise."

C35

Celine wasn't expecting anyone. The rapping of knuckles on her front door halted her typing. She peered at the door and listened as a few more light taps followed. Giving herself another minute before lifting her rump from the chair, Celine sauntered to the door and looked through the peep hole warily. She frowned seeing it was Tara on the other side of the door. Unhitching the lock and hastily twisting the knob, Celine opened the door with a distrustful leer.

"Can I help you?" she said, her face being the only part of her body stretching past the door's frame. Her body was practically wedged between Tara and the doorway as much as her robust belly would allow.

Cradling a basket filled with an assortment of diapers, baby bath towels, and other dainty items wrapped with a mint green, lacey material that gave just enough sheerness to view the gifts it carried, Tara wore a pleasant smile that made Celine want to gag. However she loved gifts. For that reason alone, Celine decided to give Tara the opportunity to explain why she was unexpectedly at her door.

"I wanted to talk to you. I think we should clear the air."

Celine snickered.

"We're going to have to work things out one way or another, Celine. I'm trying to be the bigger person in this ordeal. Already you're testing my patience."

Celine gave a sardonic laugh. "Is this your way of working things out? Oh please, honey, you're fooling yourself with this superiority complex."

"I never said I was superior."

She laughed again. "You don't have to say a word. You won. Your modest-Muslim act worked. I, however, see the real you."

Celine could see tension building in Tara's cheeks as her eyes twitched and her features tightened. It was enjoyable.

"I'm not pretending to be anything, Celine. I think you're mad with the wrong person."

"Once again you're pretending to be clueless," Celine said. "I'm not mad at you or Umar. Both of you are poor examples of what the beautiful religion of Islam teaches. He had sex and got a woman pregnant he wasn't married to then moved on to marry another woman. You are enabling such a distasteful behavior with your eyes and your heart pathetically wide open refusing to accept the reality that Umar is not husband material."

Tara's body leaned away and stiffened. Celine smirked. She'd struck a nerve.

"You can think whatever you'd like about us but it won't change anything. You're going to be upset, bitter, and alone if you want to hoard anger."

"Should I not be angry?"

"You can choose to be whatever helps you sleep at night. I just came to bring you something; a gift for the baby." Tara bent down and put the basket on the floor in front of the door. "I can see nothing will get accomplished today." She then turned and trekked down the hall towards the emergency exit.

"We don't need your gift." Seething at the thought of Tara trying to make a mockery of her pregnancy by dropping off a gift and rubbing she and Umar's proposal in Celine's pudgy face, Celine snatched the basket from the floor and traced Tara's footsteps. "You can tell Umar we don't need anything from him or you."

Tara pushed towards the door. "Go back inside, Celine, you're acting crazy and you're pregnant."

Bubbling even more with rage and refusing to be dismissed, Celine hitched her speed ready to throw the basket at Tara's pretty-little head. Tara crossed the doorway and entered the exit. Fuming, Celine followed and jogged down the staircase.

"I hope you two have a nice life," she said, pulling the basket back ready to heave it.

Celine slipped.

Feet flying in the air, back crashing to the ground, Celine landed on her side colliding with the cemented staircase. She screamed painfully exhausting every ounce of air in her lungs. The impact of her head smacking against the hard floor and her back plowing to the ground, sent a searing stab to her spine. Bawling in pain, Celine cried for help as the warm sensation of a liquidity substance began to leak from her body, seeping through her shorts.

"Oh my goodness, subhan'Allah, you're bleeding," Tara cried.

Celine tried to lift her body but the pain was too strong. Mild contractions tore though her belly and the bleeding progressed. Tara whipped out her cell and called for help.

"It's going to be okay, Celine. Ya Allah."

"My baby," Celine screamed.

"It's going to be okay," Tara combed through Celine's hair rhythmically with her sobbing.

Tara gave the operator directions and an overview of what was going on. Her calm words did not yield Celine's tears. She knew she was going to lose the baby. There were two months left in her pregnancy and for the first time ever she found herself crying to Allah for help. Blood seemed to gush from her insides endlessly until paramedics rushed up the stairs with a stretcher.

36

"The baby will have to stay in the hospital for a short while but she'll be okay, in shaa Allah," Umar said. He sat in a chair next to Celine's hospital bed holding a book with Arabic writing on the cover.

Celine squinted as her eyes adjusted to the light and pulled the covers over her chest, making herself comfortable. The pain meds were wearing off. She had fallen into a deep sleep after labor, the best sleep she'd remembered having in months. How was she supposed to react to the day's events? Did Umar know that her effort to attack Tara ultimately lead to the premature delivery of their baby? It was her fault that their little girl was strapped to an incubator learning how to breath, underweight, and introduced to the world before her time.

Celine reached for the cup of ice water next to her bed that Umar so kindly had waiting for her. It was one of the things she'd told him was his job to make sure she had plenty of during her labor. He did as promised.

Taking a sip then lowering it back to the table Celine took a moment to take it all in. She wanted to see her baby, yet guilt told her to wait. She could not handle it.

"I'm sorry," she whispered shamefully.

"You did great, Celine, what are you sorry for?"

He didn't know. The innocence and calm to his voice indicated Tara kept their confrontation a secret. Umar had a temper and although he would've tried his best to remain calm, he wouldn't dare pretend to be clueless.

"For the baby being born so early," she said.

"Qadr of Allah. There's nothing to be sorry about. She's a fighter, like her mother," he smiled, "in shaa Allah everything will work itself out."

"In shaa Allah," Celine said and smiled back.

"Would you like to see her?"

"No."

"No?"

"Not yet," she said. "Do you mind going to my apartment and gathering some things? This hospital gown is very uncomfortable and I can't imagine what my hair and makeup looks like."

"This isn't the time to be worried about your hair and makeup, rest up."

"I will," she said, "I promise."

"Good."

There was an uncomfortable distance between them. For being two new parents this moment should've been grand. A huge blessing. Celine just couldn't force herself to jump for joy. Umar was not hers, the baby was sick, and things seemed to be getting worse by the day. Tears rose to the corners of her eyes.

"Are you okay?" Umar asked, rubbing her shoulder. "Celine, maybe if you see the baby you'll understand she really is well."

"It's not that."

"What's wrong?"

"This is just too much for me to handle. Can you leave now, please?"

"I don't understand."

"Of course you don't. This is not how things are supposed to be but look how you're making them."

"Calm down, Celine, let's not do this right now. We should be celebrating our newborn, not fighting over relationship problems."

Celine gulped and turned on her side. It was easy for him to say. Easy for Umar to ignore the happenings of her life and turn it into another one of Celine's ludacris requests. She wasn't insane for being upset with him or her life, as of now.

"Have you called my mother?"

"Yes," he said from behind her back, "she sounded so happy. You should call her when you feel up to it."

"I will."

"What should we name her?"

Celine ignored him.

"We never discussed the details of nursing, names, or aqeekah-"

"I read about them in the book you gave me," she said coldly.

"Masha Allah."

"Get the wheelchair so I can visit her, please?"

"Of course I will, anything else?"

"Is Tara here?"

"No, she called me and said you fell down the stairs."

"Did she tell you what happened?"

"We didn't have time to discuss it. You were being rushed to the hospital, but I'm sure you can fill me in."

"Hmph,"

"Is there something I should know?"

Celine turned back to Umar. "Did you send her to my apartment? It was odd for her to come unexpected."

"We'd thought it was a good idea for you two to talk."

Celine frowned. "Do you enjoy torturing me? How could you think it would be a good idea, Umar? You're extremely inconsiderate towards my feelings. Please leave. It's your fault I delivered early."

"You're not going to blame things on me, Celine. This is getting old."

Celine pressed the button on her bed and called for a nurse. "Come back tomorrow."

"I'm staying the night. You may not like it but this is a new start for us. We will learn to get along and be good parents to our child." It was something about way he scolded her that sent chills through her body. Secretly, she loved it.

Umar took his phone out and showed Celine a picture.

"She's beautiful, Celine, and looks a lot like you."

She did. Dark sleek hair laid perfectly against her cream skin. Her eyes took after Celine's Cambodian side but her lips were those of Umar's. Celine cooed at the picture wishing she could hold her in her arms.

"She's gorgeous, Umar," she exclaimed proudly.

"I told you, just like her mother."

Celine continued to adore the baby's picture.

"My family will be here shortly. Everyone's excited about the new addition."

"That's wonderful."

"They're praying for her health."

"Umar," Celine said, "I know this is not the time, but think about our family before you do something you may live to regret. Don't you realize how beautiful of a moment this is between us? We may never share days like this again if you marry another woman."

Umar nodded. "My feelings haven't changed, Celine, I'm sorry."

C37

Back at the office things weren't looking too good by the look on Rashid's face. Rashid, accompanied by two other men, were stationed in Rashid's office awaiting Umar's arrival. He'd left the hospital after his talk with Celine eager to show Rashid and his co-workers pictures of his baby girl. Only the mood in the large office was gloomy and cramped, telling Umar that there was a storm wafting his way.

"Take a seat," Rashid said.

Umar walked to the third chair opposite Rashid; next to the two men. The one seated closest to him was an African American man with a trimmed beard and a navy suit with a white and plaid tie hanging from his neck. Umar thought the man's sense of style was like his own and felt less threatened by his presence. The other was a fair skinned, Caucasian male with a long red beard, a white thobe, matching kufi, and a hard scowl fixed tightly to his face. Both of the men possessed familiar faces from several charity banquets, though at the time Umar couldn't remember their names. What he did recall was their authoritative positions within AME. They were higher on the chain than Rashid—much higher.

"First let me say congratulations on your newborn baby," Rashid said.

"Mabrook," both of the men replied in unison.

Antsy, Umar's eyes surveyed their faces, and said, "Shukron."

"Afwan," they all unexcitedly replied.

"May we start by saying that you've done some wonderful work for this company, Umar?" The man in the navy suit said. "You've put in a lot of the groundwork and you have also assisted with some very successful campaigns. We're proud of the contributions that you've made as well as sacrifices on behalf of AME."

His partner nodded. Rashid's gaze was lowered to the desk. Umar winced at Rashid, then respectfully refocused on the man in the navy suit.

"Thank you, sir."

"No, thank you," he said.

"Brother," the other man barged in, "we've been told you're interested in joining SFN, alhumdullah, being offered such a great position is an honor."

Umar curtly nodded and nervously ran his moist hands over his denim pants. "Once again, thank you for all of the support."

The conversation bounced back to the man in blue. They were playing good cop-bad cop, obviously. Umar shot a glance to Rashid again who still neglected to make eye contact with him.

"We don't want to hold you back from your dreams, Umar, you're being released early from AME."

"Why?" Umar blurted. He knew it was coming by their shady body language, but hearing he was being fired was still a painful punch.

The man in blue, unbothered by Umar's disappointment, crossed his leg and clasped his fingers into a loose fist. "Your recent popularity on social networks pointing out very questionable relationships you've had in your personal life has been brought to our attention."

"I don't understand what my personal life has to do with AME," he said.

"It has everything to do with AME when you have a reputation as well as the company's to represent. We're a Muslim organization." Rashid butted in.

"Were you behind this, Rashid?"

"No, Umar, this matter was brought to me. I told you a few months ago to be mindful of what you're doing. I'm not the only one with eyes on this company and the employees. We have investors. Bad news travels fast."

"Fast indeed," the one in the kufi said.

"Pictures of you with numerous women has gained a lot of unwanted attention and emails from our supporters inquiring and suggesting that we support this type of behavior. You're not married, yet, you have a pregnant girlfriend and recently pictures of you and another woman have surfaced. We're excited that you're finally taking the leap into marriage, but you're zina has already been spray painted for the world to see. It's very distasteful."

Grinding on his teeth to avoid confrontation which would inevitably make things worst, Umar's knees knocked impatiently.

"You have a great resume to take with you to SFN. Let's look at the upside of this and say, alhumdullah."

Daggers the size of a shotgun fired at the man.

"However," the one in blue added, "we'll have to withdraw our recommendation for SFN. I'm sorry, brother, but we can't endorse inappropriate behavior. If you take those kinds of theatrics to another network the owners will say, 'this is who the Muslims sent us?' We're more than an entertainment company, Umar, I'm sure you already understand we represent the ummah as well."

"Yes," he grumbled, "I understand."

The one in navy stood. "Good." On cue all the men stood to shake Umar's hand. "I'm glad we could end this like gentleman, masha Allah."

Umar shook each one of their hands holding onto Rashid's longer than the others.

"As salaamu alaikum, Umar." They each greeted him one by one.

With one last final glare at Rashid, Umar humbily replied, "Wa alaikum salaam."

C38

The small walima was an elegant ceremony with purple and gold decorations, a small party of fifty attendees, and lots of food. The imam spoke briefly about the importance of marriage, family, and community just before Umar slid a beautiful two-carat platinum diamond ring on Tara's finger for her dowry. It cost him a pretty penny, one he couldn't afford to spare at the time, but nonetheless he wanted to make Tara feel as close to a queen as he possibly could. Initially she wanted to cancel the walima and schedule it for another time. Compromising and cutting the guest list in half stung his ego, but Umar was still pleased with the outcome. Newly laid off and having to enter a new marriage on unemployment was taking a toll on him. He prayed on the marriage day in and day out. Eventually he concluded it would be best for him to go through with it and leave their finances in Allah's hands.

Deep down he feared Tara was not ready for all he brought to the table. Celine had been nothing short of dramatic since she'd been home from the hospital, Umar was laid off, and even though she seemed eager and willing to contribute to the wedding, they'd had several mild disagreements since the day she paid for her own gown.

The cream gown with a large purple bow tied around her back and a purple hijab made Tara look like a princess. He gawked at his new wife as she leaned over the hotel room's balcony. There wasn't enough money for a honeymoon, just a relaxing weekend in Center City at a five-star hotel. The cool fall breeze traveled through the air, flapping Tara's hijab and dress in the wind. It was a scene from a movie. Umar walked behind Tara, grabbed her by the waist, and pressed his lips to the cloth covering her neck. Slowly gliding his hands up her curvy sides and over her shoulders, Umar removed two pins from her scarf.

"Leave it on," she whispered.

Umar pressed his pelvis closer to her rear, and said, "No."

They both laughed.

One by one he unpinned her hijab then slid it from her head. Lavish dark brown strands of hair fell to her shoulders. Umar rain his fingers through her tresses and then took Tara's chin in his hands. Passionately, he softly merged his lips with hers, using his lips to wedge her mouth open, and diving in for a deep kiss.

The two entangled their tongues and melted into each other for the first time. Fire ripped between the two, impatiently undressing all the while never parting lips. With nothing but her undergarments left to remove, Tara pulled back, stepped through the glass sliding doors, and headed to the bedroom. Craving every bit of her body, Umar, aroused beyond measure, quickly followed.

Three hours and a long nap later, the room's phone rang jolting them out of their sleep. Tara reached for the phone but Umar gently pulled her arm back, nestled against her back, and offered several kisses to her neck. He didn't want any interruptions, not even from room service. Food could wait.

"Let it ring," he firmly ordered in an erotic baritone.

Tara wiggled slightly out of his grasp.

"I don't believe in letting it ring, Umar, it could be important."

"More important than this?" he asked pressing harder against her and giving another kiss to her neck.

Ignoring him, Tara answered the phone and put it to her ear. Umar continued to peck at her neck, making Tara shutter and squirm until she urgently held her hand high insisting for him to stop.

Launching herself upward, Tara snapped the covers back. "What?"

Umar sat up as well.

"I'll be down in two minutes, thank you," she said, hurrying to her suitcase. Tara feverously rummaged through the bag, seized a blue abaya, slipped it on, removed a random scarf and carelessly wrapped it around her.

"What's wrong?"

Stepping into a pair of shoes, Tara looked too upset to answer him. "My car," she said.

Umar slid from the bed. "What's wrong with your car?"

The evil look Tara stabbed him with said more than enough and warned him to back off, but he wouldn't. She was now his wife and any matters that concerned her needed to go through him, first.

"I asked what's wrong with your car, Tara?"

Tara stopped her frenzied purse searching dash around the room and took a deep breath before addressing Umar.

"All of my car windows have been broken, Umar."

"Huh?"

"Vandalized."

"Who would do something like that?"

Tara groaned then shrieked at his question. "You know exactly who, Umar. A crazed woman with a ton of unbalanced pregnancy hormones that's furious with her daughter's father's marriage."

"You shouldn't assume without any proof, Tara. I don't think she would do something so extreme."

Tara laughed as if to say he was nothing more than a fool. "Women do it daily. All kinds of women, Umar, any race and any class; women are crazy, period, and will do anything within their power to remind you of it."

Umar walked to his bag and began getting dressed. "Let me handle it," he said.

"No."

"No?"

"I have to fill out a police report, Umar, there's nothing you can do."

Finished dressing, Umar grabbed a waist-length olive trench coat from the back of a chair, put it on, then walked to Tara extending his arms to hug and calm her down. She rejected it. Dodging his arms and circling around him.

"Now is not the time," she spat.

"Don't tell the police her name, Tara, that's not how we do things. Let's talk to Celine first."

She gasped. "What are you expecting her to say, Umar?"

"The truth."

"Is this how things are going to be? Her word versus mine?"

Tara was giving him a headache. Celine may have very well bashed out her windows, and Tara had every reason to assume such and be overly frustrated, but Umar refused to jump to conclusions.

"What if you're wrong, Tara." He remained calm. "If you're wrong, and I'm not saying that you are, but if you are you'll possibly damage Celine's chance to stay in the country. Remember she's on probation and I'm not moving to Africa anymore, Celine and the baby need to be here."

Tara's face was tight as a bear trap. Nostrils flaring and chest moving up and down, Tara took short breaths and stood silent.

"Just give a report that's good enough for the insurance company. I'm asking for you to leave Celine out of it. You'll receive the same compensation with or without her name. Let's do the best thing we can do as Muslims to be fair in this situation."

Grimacing, Tara gave Umar a long look, then sashayed off slamming the door behind her.

C39

Baby Noora was wrapped in a lavender blanket suckling from Celine's bosom when Umar entered the apartment. Celine insisted he'd keep the key she'd given him months back just in case there was ever an emergency, and also he was the closest and only family that she and Noora had in Philadelphia. Noora changed his life. Her silky, curly dark strands of hair, round cheeks, and beautiful eyes brought a new sense of love and compassion that he'd never felt, not even for Tara. He didn't know what he was thinking when he told Celine he would move to Africa and she to Canada. There wasn't a day that passed Umar didn't stop by or video chat with Celine to make sure his baby girl was okay. It was a love unlike any other, and he thanked Allah for her and prayed to keep her safe every time the precious face popped into his mind.

Things had been going well between he and Celine, very well. The transition into parenthood and co-parenting had been a lot easier than he'd predicted. She allowed him to visit and help with the baby offering little resistance or questioning his decisions. Celine never spoke of Tara or the wedding. She'd given up on nagging him about reviving their relationship and seemed to come to an acceptance of their new relationship. With her new change of attitude, Umar was terribly confused if he should even question if she in fact had anything to do with Tara's car being vandalized. It just didn't seem like something she'd do, at this time. Umar also didn't want to ruffle any feathers, instantly causing a ruckus and resulting in Celine actually doing something immature and vengeful over being upset of the accusation. It was a touchy subject.

Another thing that he'd noticed was Celine was very distant. Cold. Not in an evil way, she seemed down and slightly unaware of her surroundings, particularly when the baby would cry or need to be changed. Of course she'd get to Noora, eventually, but often times there was a definite time lapse between the baby's cry and her urge to satisfy whatever need Noora desired. A part of him attributed her lackadaisical ways as her breaking the baby in and not wanting to spoil her. Tara, on the other hand, who was a nurse was highly concerned about Celine and possibly post partum depression. If Tara was correct, which Umar hoped she wasn't, Celine may rightfully been a suspect for bashing Tara's windows.

"How's she doing today, well, in shaa Allah?" Umar crossed the living room and took Noora from Celine's arms. Resting her head in the bend of his arm, he kissed Noora gently and gave the baby the greeting.

Celine ran her fingers through her mismanaged hair and slumped into the chair. "She's been crying all day," she said.

Hardly acknowledging Celine's somber deportment, Umar took a seat on the sofa and rocked the baby, stroking her head in tiny circles.

"She behaves a lot better when she's with you," Celine said. "Maybe you should take her for a few days."

"I can on Friday. Technically I'm still on my honeymoon."

He waited for a reaction. "You wouldn't believe what happened."

"Surprise me?"

"Someone vandalized Tara's car."

"Oh,"

"Oh?"

"Hmph," she said indifferently, then stood and walked slowly to the kitchen. "I didn't know she had so many enemies."

"She doesn't."

"Obviously she does."

He could hear her fumbling around in the refrigerator and then in the cabinets.

"She thinks it was you."

Celine reentered the living room clutching a wine glass filled to the brim. She took a sip. "I'm sorry to hear that, she's wrong."

"Have you been drinking?"

"No," she said and batted her lashes with a sharp eye roll. "Since you're taking the baby back with you I am now."

"I clearly said I couldn't. Besides you can't drink and breastfeed."

She sucked her teeth. "I've decided today would be the last day for that."

"You agreed to two years like the sunnah."

"When I agreed I didn't know she'd do a fine job of shredding my nipples and exhausting all of my energy. I'm tired, Umar, something you wouldn't understand because you've been partying downtown with your new bride."

He didn't know where this was coming from. Minutes before he revered over their new ability to co-parent, somehow they'd quickly found their way back to the good ole days.

Not wanting to upset the baby, Umar decided to let Celine win. "Fine," he said, "If you would like to stop breastfeeding that is entirely up to you. It's your body."

"It sure is."

"I'm just asking the next decision you'll make that effects our child's health can I please be informed and consulted with first."

She shrugged.

"Thanks," he said.

Celine swallowed another sip. "I did it, Umar."

Bringing the rocking to a pause, Umar gazed at Celine, and said, "Did what?"

"Bashed her windows. All of them. I was upset."

Bewildered, Umar stared at Celine disappointedly. "I can't believe you'd do something so crazy."

"Both of you can afford to fix it," she said and lifted her shoulders, cupping the glass while giggling and sipping all at once. "Two incomes are better than one."

"We can't afford to just fix things, Celine, I was laid off. Are we back to the impulsive tantrums?"

"No," she said, "because I need to get back to the old me. I need to work on Celine and I have very little time to be held back by the distractions that you offer in my life."

"What does that mean?"

She tapped her fingers on her lips, juggling her thoughts before speaking. "I want you to keep her," she said.

"Keep her?"

"Yes. You were one-hundred percent correct about Canada being the best place for me. You have a wife now and the perfect opportunity to raise Noora in a way that I never had and I cannot offer her. She's young enough to accept Tara as her own."

"I don't believe what I'm hearing." Umar suckled the baby close and stood to his feet, walking to the bedroom.

"I've thought long and hard about this," she said, "it's what's best."

He didn't want to hear another word nor was he interested in playing a game with Celine. This would not be his life. She would not play with him like a puppet, pulling strings as she pleased, and Celine would not have the pleasure of seesawing with Noora either.

"I don't want you to take your words back. This is your decision and I won't allow you to teeter-totter. Remember this is what you asked for, Celine."

When he turned his back from packing the baby's bag Celine was posted against the doorway. "You're not going to give me a chance to discuss this."

He wanted to strangle her. He yearned to curse and yell and tell her she was the biggest mistake of his life, but she wasn't. Celine was the mother of his child and by the will of Allah a great blessing. This was life.

"There's nothing to discuss, Celine. We can play games with each other and you can cause a ton of corruption in my life, but not in Noora's."

She began sobbing, but Umar was unaffected by her tears.

"If you'd like to see her you can call. I'll file for custody and I don't need your support. Just please do me a favor?" he said. "Find your way to Allah."

Her blank expression told him she was not expecting such a neutral response from him, and she was biting her own tongue. It would've been easy for Umar to fuss and force her to be a parent, but inside he knew what was best. Inside he knew Celine was not expecting to have a baby or any of the hardships that came along with it; she was expecting to have a man. A man that would fill her void of companionship and relevance in this world. Little did she know, the void she'd felt was one that no man on this earth could fill. Not her father, and for sure, not Umar.

C40

"I'm sorry," Umar said, placing Noora's car seat on the hotel room's floor.

Eyes wide and confused, Tara held her hands high with a copy of the police report in her hand. "Why is Noora here, Umar, what's going on?"

Umar kneeled before Tara and held her hands. Kissing the back of them, he used the back of her hand to caress his cheek. "I'm sorry, Tara, and I understand if you want to get out of this marriage before it starts."

Swiftly snatching her hand away, Tara jumped to her feet. "What are you talking about? What are you sorry for?"

"For bringing you into this mess. This hasn't been easy for you and you have been more than patient with everything I bring to the table. The drama with Celine, me losing my job, and now this," he said pointing to Noora who was sleeping soundly in the car seat. He dropped the diaper bag from his shoulder to the ground.

"I don't understand, Umar, this," she said aiming a finger at the baby, "is your daughter. And this," she said, waving her finger and pointing at she and Umar, "is our honeymoon."

"I know. I tried to talk to Celine while you handled everything with your car. I planned to get to the bottom of things and make it easy as possible for both of us, but she decided she couldn't handle the baby anymore."

"What?"

"I know, this is a lot to handle."

"What does she plan to do?"

"Move to Canada and get her life together, I guess."

Tara darted to the car seat and removed Noora. Cradling her against her chest, she squeezed the innocent baby and kissed her forehead. "Is this a joke of hers?"

"I'm not sure."

"Ya Allah, what is wrong with the people?"

"I don't want to burden you," he said.

"You're my husband, Umar, this is the will of Allah."

"I know but I also understand if this will be too much."

She squeezed the baby again. "She isn't a burden, Umar. This is a shock but not a burden."

"I think Celine is going through some things and just needs to get her life together. I don't want the stress of shifting through her feelings as she figures them out day to day."

"She has to see her child, Umar."

"Yes, I know. Right now I just want to give her time."

"I'm speechless."

"Again," he said, "I'm sorry."

Tara walked over to the bed and sat. Silently soothing the baby, she and Umar held little Noora's hand's, ogling at her beauty. There was so much to say, yet neither of them said anything.

"She looks like her mother," Tara finally said.

"Masha Allah,"

"I'll never be her mother, Umar. She needs her mother. I can only be a great example."

"I know this," he said, sadly.

"But I will love her and take care of her like she is my own. I'll promise you that, in shaa Allah."

"In shaa Allah," he whispered

A year ago Umar would've never seen this coming. His life was no longer his own and he'd truly realized it was not in his hands. Blow after blow he'd learn to take whatever came his way. There was no other choice. Though it seemed like a hardship, this new lifestyle bestowed on him was a blessing. He didn't have to endure it alone. Allah had blessed Umar with a beautiful, loving, and understanding wife that was willing to maneuver through the storm with him. For that, he was grateful. Inside, he knew Celine would come back around, and when she did he told himself that he'd take her in with open arms. As much as he hated to admit, there were other options. Instead, he chose to please himself and not his maker.

Celine only participated in what she believed to be normal, and she only wanted the things that any woman in this life deserved- a kind husband, friend, and family. She wasn't insane for wanting those things. There was nothing absurd about it.

Umar took Noora out of Tara's arms and cuddled her against his chest. He'd failed her. He failed Celine and he also failed Tara. He did, however, have a chance to make things better for his baby girl, and in shaa Allah he'd devote the rest of his life to doing just that.

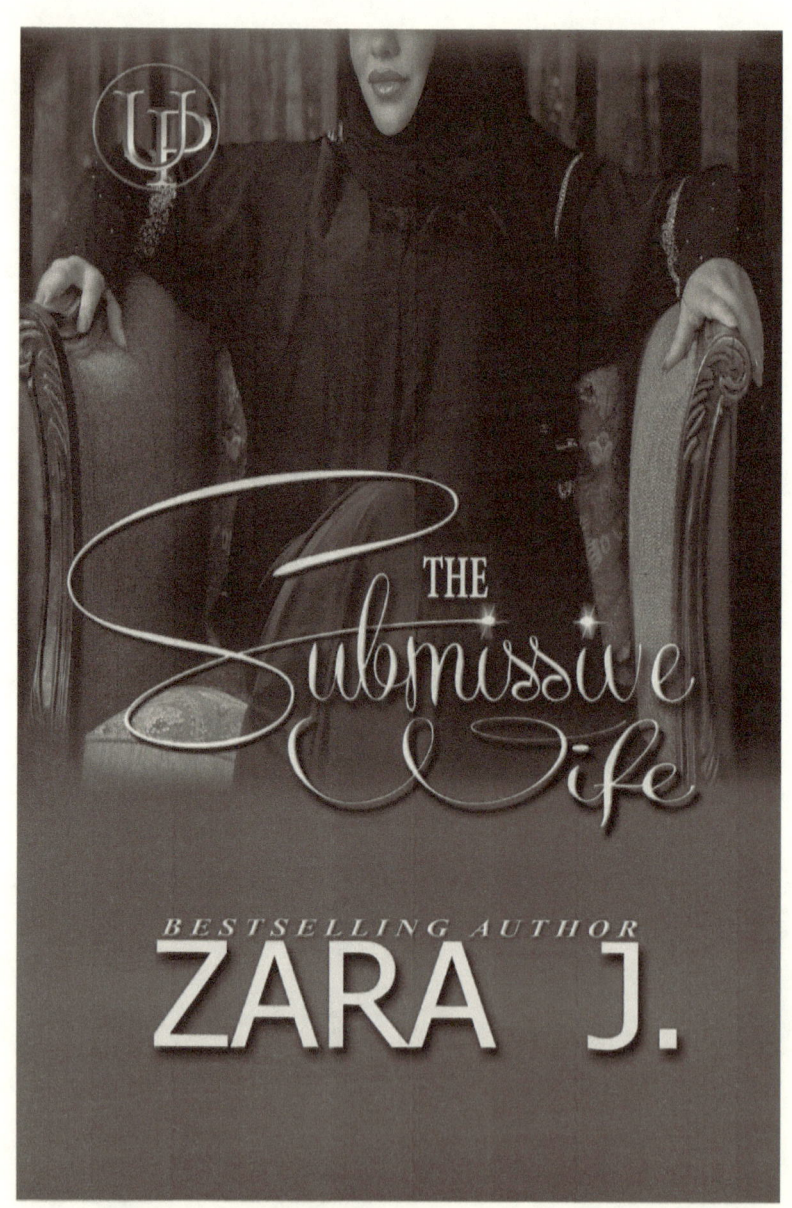

THE
Submissive
Wife

BESTSELLING AUTHOR
ZARA J.

The Submissive Wife

Something was extremely strange. Usually when I entered the den where my husband, Lateef, entertained guests I'd have to quickly shy away and scurry out of the room due to the overwhelming currant of testosterone waving throughout the room. Tonight was different. From the moment I strutted into the room, securely towing a silver tray covered with an assortment of raisin glazed biscuits, homemade triple chocolate cake, chi tea, and a few sugar-free, vegan cookies for Lateef's diabetic friend, Paul, who carried a crooked smile and a belly that looked harder than a bowling ball, all casual conversation ceased. Brows knit, I curiously eyed Paul behind my niqab as he picked up the supposed discussion and drew my husband's attention back to him.

Hmmm. I'd always made sure to provide Paul with special treats and catered to his health condition, I didn't like his suspicious behavior, not one bit. After all, his wondering eyes were the reason I began wearing the niqab while Lateef had guests in our home. Him not having a wife and my sugar-free delicacies caused unwanted ogling that I tried to assume was not purposefully delivered on his behalf. His odd behavior, as well as Lateef's made me wish I'd added a few tablespoons of sugar to his treats.

Lateef always held these business meetings with his companions. Whatever needed to be quieted was their business. Lateef, however, was my business. Anything he was involved in which could possibly be considered semi-questionable would somehow surface and be confronted—I always made sure of that.

"Brother," Paul said, "The empty lot next to the barbershop is a goldmine. Let's not think about customer parking, it's bigger than that."

The two other men in the room nodded. With my ears fully alert, I placed the tray on the serving table and counted four plates, leisurely adding the desserts. Investment discussions were my favorite.

"I agree," Lateef added. "Not to mention with the string of dental and doctor offices opening on the street. There's a great opportunity to make a substantial amount of income from the lot. Even if you're only charging ten-dollars for three hours. I'd have to guess the lot can hold at least forty cars."

Forty cars. Quickly I calculated a twelve hour time span, divided by three, times forty cars at ten dollars a vehicle. That would be roughly sixteen-hundred dollars a day. Nearly fifty-thousand a month! My mouth began watering. This lot was too good to be true.

Before I knew it I was in la-la land. Temporarily my mind wafted to shoes and a brand new living room. No, a brand new house. With the kind of money Lateef would soon have, in shaa Allah of course, I'd need a castle for all of the fabulousness we'd acquire. Bags. I'd need a new handbag to match the line of credit I'd be issued. Gucci? Please. Tomorrow I'd make sure to invest in a Vogue Magazine and anticipate the next budding trends for the fall. By then Lateef should have the lot all squared away.

"Typically," Paul said, "The lot would be an expensive purchase, but it's owned by a brother without any family that's looking to sell it considerably low."

"We need to move quick." One of the men said.

"Yes, we do," added Lateef. "I'm surprised he didn't donate it or approach any of the city's musallah's first."

"You know how some are, many don't want to invest in business due to the risk." One of the men, a brother who was new to their gatherings chimed in. "The old man selling the lot wants to move quickly."

"I think we should move then," Lateef said. "Who's in?"

I carefully walked around the serving table and dished out the plates one by one curtly greeting each of the men as they removed a plate from my hand. All except Lateef. When I reached him there was a cold glare in his eyes and his cheekbones were pinched. I looked at the men to see if anyone noticed the dismay on his face as I had, but they appeared unbothered and ultimately delusional. I handed him the plate. He took it, and hastily I hurried back to the table to pour them tea.

Maybe he didn't want me in the room. Serving his companions was my idea, not his, but Lateef always appeared beyond grateful for my servitude. By now it was practically expected of me. Our thirteen year marriage had a ton of traditions. His monthly business socials were one of them. My determination to uphold the royal poise that my mother instilled in me at an early age to be the ideal wife, proved to be a great benefit and easily kept our marriage bonded, his business nights always ended with him being complimented for having a wonderfully, submissive wife that appeared joyful to cater to he and his friends. So what was the shady look for? Bouncing several reasons for Lateef's peculiar visage, while pouring hot water into white china and steeping the tea, I returned to my husband first. Once again, he glowered as he took the tea into his hands then quickly looked away.

Right away my muscles twitched. Hiking back to the table, my shaky, clammy hands could barely steady themselves enough to elegantly carry the remaining saucers. I gathered my breath. Relax. It was probably nothing. Just my imagination.

Paul relaxed into the recliner, one of four in the room, and extended the foot. I tried to read his expressions as well, but Paul seemingly was unaware of any tension between Lateef and I. Heck, until now I was unaware of any tension.

"This one is just for you and I, Lateef, if you're interested. I have positioned Dawud and Sam plugged with an apartment in an area that's sure to be a big boom."

"Masha Allah," Lateef said. "Okay, alhumdullah, let's get the details worked out and I'll contact my lawyer, in shaa Allah."

"Alhumdullah," they all said.

Ahumdullah. This was going to be great. We'd truly have the secured future I'd been waiting for. Sure, Lateef owned several successful businesses and a few properties, but I didn't feel secure. Not with the ever revolving second-wife door. This however, added a new layer of stability. Finally, we were on our way from being thousand-aires to millionaires. By the time I was thirty-six in shaa Allah, just three years away, I'd feel positive enough about our finances to layoff the Mirena birth control and present the world with a baby Maryam. Lying to Lateef about the IUD had become tiresome anyways, and I felt awful for doing so.

Giddily collecting the trays, I trekked out of the room and dropped them into the sink, hand washed them—because china does not go into the dishwasher, then dried them with a towel. A dab of peach lotion for my hands, removed my niqab, and then untied my apron. The boys' talk in the other room raised my brows once again. This time, it was clear something bad was brewing. I stopped. Held my breath—so not even a whisper could go unheard, and angled my body towards the den's entryway.

"Are you sure about this?" It sounded like Paul.

"What has to be done must be done," Lateef, who's voice would never go unrecognized said sullenly.

I heard the springs from the recliner pop and then feet shuffle. "I'll leave things to you three gentleman," one of the brothers said, "my wife is waiting for me and she GPS's traffic timing." They all laughed but I thought his wife was a genius. We'd need to meet one day.

"Okay," Paul said, "Let's get this over with. I really hate these things."

"Me too," Lateef said, briefly he was silent. "Unfortunately, when reality hits you must ride with the wave."

"Indeed," they all agreed.

My lips contorted as a frown formed. Waves in this house weren't rode without me. Just as I released my breath and hitched another heap of air to hold, Lateef beckoned me.

"Maryam, can you please come here so we can talk?"

My puffed chest forcefully blew out that heap of air. Wait, was I the wave? Utterly confused, heart swirling with adrenaline, and hands trembling even more than before, I walked to the counter and refastened my niqab then I sauntered to the room.

The gentleman on his way out, Sam, crossed my path, and said goodbye with a friendly, "As salaamu alaikum."

I mumbled it back. Typically I would've offered to pack a treat for his wife upon departure, but obviously my services weren't needed. Lateef's summon was far more important and the eavesdropping made the circumstance very uncomfortable.

Lateef stood.

"Maryam," he said, pointing to the now empty recliner, "take a seat."

Embarrassed and muddled, I cupped my hands, forged a grin that only my eyes revealed, and did as I was told.

DOWRY
DIVAS

CAN YOU PUT A PRICE ON LOVE?

ZARA J.

KHADIJAH'S GOT HER Groove

F.A. IBRAHIM

Her
JUSTICE

NASHEED JAXSON